SECOND
COMING

SECOND COMING

A NOVEL

ROBERT HOLMES

MILL CITY PRESS

Mill City Press, Inc.
2301 Lucien Way #415
Maitland, FL 32751
407.339.4217
www.millcitypress.net

Printed in the United States of America.

Library of Congress Control Number: 2020904592

ISBN-13: 978-1-6312-9023-7

DEDICATION

To my wife, Diane, whose presence makes me darn near perfect!
To my son, Matt, who inspired me; and to my daughters, Aletha
and Abi, who cheered me on. With Love and Gratitude always.

AUTHOR BIOGRAPHY

B ob Holmes is a retired educator and Human Resources manager. He has graduate degrees in Education and Social Science and served for 20 years as an elected member of his regional school committee. Bob originally planned to be a professional historian; he has a degree in Early American History from the College of William and Mary, in Williamsburg, Virginia, and has pursued history as an avocation throughout his life. He and his wife, Diane, have lived in their colonial farmhouse in Western Rhode Island for over 40 years. Here, where two of their three children were born at home, they raised all three kids and maintained a small farm. Bob is a collector of all things old and interesting and has involved his three grandchildren in his various hobbies. One of those hobbies is writing, and thus this book. Currently, he and Diane are enjoying their role as grandparents and their life as retirees.

PROLOGUE

"It's a minor miracle! They've granted us access to the Shroud!" Dr. John Baptista, head of the University's Genetics Program here in Boston, was genuinely surprised. He had honestly not expected this - indeed, he had steeled himself for disappointment. Based on their considerable correspondence with the Vatican and given the Church's lack of even a modicum of encouragement, he had presumed the answer would be no. After all, It had been decades since anyone had been allowed scientific study of the Shroud, and there had undoubtedly been numerous requests that were either ignored or turned away. He had actually expected a long wait and a final refusal. Instead, this unexpected and rather fast approval. Why was HIS request granted, and why now? He had no idea.

He quickly scanned the one-page letter to see if it had an answer. None that he could discern. It contained only a direct confirmation that the Holy Father, the Pope himself, had approved their request to study the shroud with up-dated scientific methodology. Conditions would, of course, apply - those that had already been tentatively accepted by the team, and perhaps one or two more to come. The research would be done in complete secrecy, findings reported exclusively to the Papal office, only non-destructive examination of the cloth itself. A representative of the Pope would be present at all times while the Shroud was being examined. That was it. Not a word about why permission was granted or what His Holiness expected them to find or report. Signed by the Papal Secretary with a hand-written note that someone from Rome would be in Boston to meet with them in the next few days.

Dr. Baptista shook his head and passed the letter over to his two colleagues seated at the office coffee table. The excitement in the room was electric. Dr. Renee Josephson, the University's top Bio-Chemist, felt a rush of emotions: Joy, relief, anticipation, perhaps even a hint of anxiety; but mostly pure, child-like delight. She would be an integral part of the great challenge that had been granted them - a challenge they had eagerly sought and which now presented itself, in her quite brilliant mind, as a mountain to be climbed, or a maze to be negotiated. The joy was in the doing - working through the puzzle, examining each piece, fitting them together until a picture begins to emerge. Making sense of things. Understanding. She held the letter, focused on the Papal Arms, on the keys. Yes, this letter was the key to a potentially wonderful adventure of the mind, an exercise in pure science, and she was already anxious to get started.

She passed the letter on to Marty Thomas, who took it from her, dropped the glasses from his forehead onto his nose, examined it, then read it slowly and carefully. Dr. Thomas was a serious sceptic, and he was looking for any sign or nuance that would in any way contradict the letter's authenticity or it's straight-forward content. He was pleased to find none. Yes, the letter appeared genuine and it appeared to give them all that they had asked for in terms of access and process. Nonetheless, he already had a nagging sense that all was not as simple as it seemed, that perhaps they were being pulled into a game they didn't know they were playing. He shook the feeling off. Game or not, Doctor Thomas was up for it and he couldn't help sensing the excitement build as he thought about applying his radiological skills to the quest for an answer. Just who was this fellow, Jesus of Nazareth?

CHAPTER 1

I t would be an extraordinary meeting. Father Paul McCormack had been summoned for a personal audience with His Holiness, an unscheduled, and as far as he'd been told, a very private meeting as well. When thePapal Secretary had called, he'd expected, perhaps, a few final instructions before he headed out of the Vatican for his flight to Boston. He knew, of course, from his previous meetings with the Secretary that what he was doing was potentially significant, both to the Church and to himself personally. He knew that he had the authority of the Holy See and that the Holy Father had approved what he was beginning to think of as his pilgimage. But his instructions had been vague, limited to "meet with, facilitate, monitor and report." Perhaps now he would get more detail, some guidance or direction, from the Pope himself. Paul had only had general audiences with the Pope during his several years in Rome, so it was not surprising that he felt a tinge of anxiety, but that feeling was overwhelmed by one of anticipation as he was ushered into the Papal Residence.

As he waited in the anteroom for his audience to begin, McCormack found himself thinking fondly of the Holy Father. John Paul III had been elevated to the Throne a bit more than a year ago, the first African to fill the Shoes of the Fisherman, a remarkable man with real promise to be a remarkable leader. His ministry had always been about one thing: Redemption for the "little people," and not just Catholics, or even Christians, but all God's children.

1

McCormack found that, in itself, refeshing and endearing. No one really knew yet where this Pope would lead the Church, but there was little doubt that he would do whatever he could to make the world a kinder and more Christian place. He had seen incredible poverty and more death by disease, hunger and outright violence than anyone deserved to be exposed to in a lifetime, and he was resolute in his intention to bring an end to the reign of the Four Horsemen. His election was not completely unexpected, although there had been several other candidates with strong resumes. Perhaps their ambition had gotten in the way, or perhaps their conservative theology was an impediment. He, himself, was a man of grace and quiet dignity, exuding personal warmth and empathy. In short, he had a special kind of charisma that was a perfect fit with the role he had taken on, and it was easily recognized by the other Cardinals. He had made no special effort to seek high office, yet his election had come quickly. Although not young, he was the youngest to become Bishop of Rome in hundreds of years. His selection was widely applauded and it was anticipated that he would occupy the Seat for a long and effective reign. He had taken the name John Paul because he wanted to demonstrate his spiritual connection to an admired predecessor and because he wanted his name to proclaim his mission...

The clicking of a door latch interrupted McCormack's train of thought; the door swung open to reveal a large, not-quite-informal, but certainly less than regal, meeting room. John Paul sat at the far side of the room, clearly comfortable, in a large red leather easy chair. But for his clerical vestments, Father McCormack thought, he could easily have been mistaken for one of the priest's graduate school mentors at Notre Dame. He felt instantly at ease. The Holy Father motioned for Paul to approach, and, as he did, he dropped to one knee and touched his lips to the ring on the pope's finger. McCormack saw the crossed keys of Peter in full relief and he experienced a brief moment of awe. Still not having spoken a word, His Holiness motioned McCormack to a smaller, but comfortable, chair separated from the Pope by an ornate coffee table. Father McCormack sat and waited...

It was only a moment before the Pope, speaking clear Oxford English, said, "Father McCormack, it is a pleasure to meet you; you know, of course, that I have chosen you to be my personal emissary on what could prove to be an exhilarating and potentially risky pilgrimage of mind and spirit. What you do not know is why I have chosen you, or how I have decided to embark on this task. Why I have chosen you is easy: Among a few well-educated and talented young men who were recommended for my consideration, you alone are a scientist, an American, you speak fluent Italian and Spanish, and you apparently share much of my vision for our Church. I am told by your superiors that you can be trusted to carry out your mission in complete secrecy and report only to me. Is this so?"

McCormack nodded and said, "Yes, Holliness, you can have complete confidence in me."

"Good, good. I had no doubt, but wanted to secure your personal confirmation. What I am asking you to do will probably be a great burden both of work and to your faith; I trust you are also willing to confirm that commitment?"

McCormack nodded again; the Pope nodded in response.

"Alright, then. Now the more difficult question to answer is why I am sending you on this quest. In the simplest terms, I believe God has spoken to me and suggested this course. Miraculous? No, I don't think so. A revelation? Perhaps. More likely, a bit of Divine guidance. Yes, Divine Guidance in the form of dreams. Allow me to explain. Shortly after my election, I began to have dreams - recurring dreams - about the Turin Shroud. At first they were unfocused, but over a few weeks time they began to crystalize. I was alone in Turin Cathedral, a pilgrim before the shroud. I could clearly see the face of our Lord and I heard Him say, quietly but distinctly, "It is time." Then, more insistently, "It is time and you must act." I puzzled over this dream for some days and had almost lost it in the way dream memories tend to fade. At just this time I had a private meeting with an old friend, the Archbishop of Boston, and in the course of our conversation he mentioned a group that wanted to re-open scientific inquiry into the Shroud. In particular, they were interested in seeking out DNA for testing and possible attribution. I knew immediately that this was, at least in part, an answer to my puzzlement. I asked him to have the prospective researchers develop a very brief proposal and forward it for my consideration. When the proposal was in hand and I saw the researcher's names, I knew what had to be done. I authorized the project. Now I will tell you the truly odd thing: I know very little of what they propose to do or hope to find, but I know it must be done. I believe it is what God wants and I believe that something important will come of it, but I remain ignorant of what that might be. Consider my commitment an article of faith, and you my champion."

McCormack wanted to ask the Pope exactly what he wanted him to do. After all, the young priest did not enjoy the kind of heavenly guidance that was apparently available to the Bishops of Rome. The Pope had made it clear that he had faith in his Divine Guidance and in what would come of it. But what, precisely, was Paul McCormack supposed to do and how was he supposed to do it? Paul felt a wavering in his confidence, but faith won out. If the Holy Father had placed His faith in Paul, who was McCormack to be a doubter? Surely the will of God would win out in the end...

"I understand, Your Holiness. Are there any specific instructions?"

John Paul was pensive for a moment. "If I were young and unencumbered by a throne I would be only too glad to have the opportunity awaiting you. I want you to meet the researchers, provide them with whatever access and financial resources they require, monitor but do not interfere with their inquiries, understand to the best of your ability what they are doing, and enable them to be successful. Yes, you are to be the enabler, acting directly for me. I will open any door, support any decision, provide any resource so long as these people have integrity and act in good conscience. This is what you must ascertain. I do not know where this will lead, only that God wants it to happen. Now go and do God's will."

The audience was over. The Pope blessed McCormack and the priest was quietly escorted out of the room. His head was spinning. How could this possibly turn out? He thought "God only knows," and smiled at the thought. Soon he would be on his way to Boston.

CHAPTER 2

The entire team had gathered to meet Father McCormack. There were five of them now, all friends, seated around a conference table in a private area of the Museum of Fine Arts. This is where two of them worked - or, perhaps better said, pursued their professional passions. They were both Art Historians of a sort, both Ph.D.s, both in research and curatorial roles here at the BFA.

Matthew Hightower was a published expert on Christian art and artifacts. He was the only member of the team who had ever actually seen the shroud in situ at Turin Cathedral. He found it to be intriguing, and in several ways rather curious. It was unquestionably significant as an apparent "Holy Relic" and the investigation and proper classification of holy relics was among his main interests. He was not especially interested in authenticating them, although authentication came within his purview. In some sense he felt they were all authentic representatives of art and history; some of them were just not what they were purported to be. He thoroughly enjoyed examining such objects and attempting to determine, as best he could, their origin and history - both as objects of art and as objects of veneration. Most of the time their stories were fascinating and they revealed a great deal about a Western World that was dominated by belief, priestly and military elites, uneducated masses, and simple art and artifacts that connected those masses and confirmed their beliefs. Of course there were the magnificant monuments to those times, most notably the great gothic cathedrals, bringing light to the Dark Ages (in a quite literal way, via their incredible stained glass windows), lifting the eyes of worshipers upward toward the high vaulted ceilings, and pointing heavenwards with their almost unimaginable spires. Were they, themselves, not proof of miracles? Paintings, statuary and frescos completed the "high art" picture, but it was the lowly relics that, as often as not, inspired the likes of Piers Plowman and were cause for pilgrimages and, consequently, enriching the churches, monestaries and chapter houses that held them. It was from this perspective that Matt Hightower viewed the shroud. He would not judge it. He would seek to understand it and set it in its proper historical and artistic perspective.

Maria Baptista was the fifth member of the team. She was the curator for Medieval, Renaissance and Baroque Art, well-known and respected for her knowledge not just of the art, but of how the art was made. She understood pigments and solvents, where they were found, how they were mixed and applied, and in what time periods and by which artisits they were used. She was intimate with the relationship between "her" paintings and the Medieval and Reanaissance Church - she knew who commissioned what kinds of work and who was capable of producing it, so that when a previously unknown work appeared, or there was need for authentication of a known one, she was one of a very few people who might be entrusted with the task. Hers was a lifetime love affair with paintings that adorned the walls of museums, churches and private collections, and with the people who had created them, the people who had used them to portray their story, and, now, the people who safeguarded and protected them. She also recognized that not all the art she loved was great art, or, perhaps, not even originally intended as "art." She thought that perhaps the shroud fell into this category, but she was unprepared to make any serious judgement until she had undertaken a thorough and proper examination. She was confident in her ability to judge pigments, but less so in her knowledge of woven cloth. She had been reading a great deal lately to enhance her understanding of warp and weave through various historical periods, but she thought that she could, at best, review previous critical judgements on that aspect of the Shroud.

In adddition to being the fifth member of the team, Maria was also Joseph Baptista's wife, or as she preferred to see it, his equal partner for life. Joe saw it the same way. They admired each other, they were friends - had been friends for years before their friendship turned to love - and they respected the demands of each other's professional life. They had been married for about ten years, shared a handsome and prestigious town house close to the Public Gardens, and loved their sophisticated, urban lifestyle. Of late there had been talk of children, the typical conversations, perhaps, of those women who are beginning to run out of child-bearing years and those men who, not yet fathers, have not quite given up on the idea. Surely a decision could wait just a little longer...certainly until they got back from Italy...

The conversation around the table had begun with talk about what to expect from McCormack. What would he be like? What kind of person would the Vatican send; how could he possibly remain neutral? Would he respect scientific inquiry? Would he help or hinder their investigation? Would he have a list of additional constraints or suggest some particular findings? They agreed that there was little use speculating; they would know soon enough. Instead, they decided to focus on costs and equipment. There was no foundation behind them, no funding source provided by believers in the shroud who were willing to pay for the proof they were certain would be uncovered. They had been unable to find a single philanthropic organization that saw any real scientific or social value in what they proposed to do. So it was up to them to provide the resources for themselves. It was not the most comfortable position to be in, but all of them were committed to the venture, and between them they could probably pull it off...

There was a knock at the door and the door opened to reveal a young priest with a gentle smile. "Good evening. I'm Paul Mcormack. It's good to be back in Boston. May I come in?"

CHAPTER 3

"**D**o come in and join us," said Maria, returning his smile. "We're delighted to meet you - and do I detect a bit of Boston in you?" Yes, he's a Boston brat, she thought, and that should make for a more comfortable meeting for everyone. Could bode well for good relations with this young fellow. And, on second look, he was not nearly as young as he appeared from a distance; that, too, bode well. She stood to meet him as he crossed the floor toward her and shook his hand. Mid to late 30s, she guessed, about the same age as Renee. She caught herself wondering if the two of them would get on. But that thought fled as she focused on introducing McCormack to the other four team members, who were now standing around their guest, hands extended. After a couple of minutes of getting-to-know-you chatter, Maria intervened. "Coffee or water anyone? No? Then let's sit down and get started. John, would you like to lead off?"

It was immediately evident to Father McCormack that John was in charge. The priest already knew that the basic proposal was John's and the team, composed of his closest professional friends, along with his wife, had formed around him. He would be the guy to go to when decisions had to be made, and he was the guy to go to now. He began:

"Well, Father, you are, I assume, familiar with our proposal?"

"Thoroughly," replied McCormack, "And, please, call me Paul. I am hopeful that informality will be our friend."

"OK, Paul. Sounds good. First names only from here on out. So you know what we plan to do and how we will do it. The big questions we have are when, and what your role will be."

Paul nodded and John continued. "To be honest, we were actually surprised to be granted access to the Shroud, but even more surprised at how quickly that approval came. To get directly to the point, we are only this evening identifying the financial resources we need. We have rather hurriedly begun to identify sources from which to borrow or use necessary equipment. Potential consultants need to be contacted. And we all need to schedule time away from work - easier for some of us than for others, but certainly not a major impediment. In short, your arrival, coming but days after the initial notification, has caught us unprepared to begin. We hope you can appreciate our problem and give us some time to get organized..."

"I can do a lot better than that," said Paul. "I certainly do appreciate your operational concerns, and let's not lose sight of the condition of secrecy. But let me assure you: I have been sent to enable your work, not to confound or present obstacles. My instructions come directly from the Holy Father. He delivered them to me in a personal audience. Let me share those instructions with you, just as he gave them to me. I am to do whatever is required to fully enable your work. I am to provide the resources, open the doors, and see to it that you have everything you need. I am not to intervene in your research in any way. I am to monitor and report to His Holiness, but with the understanding that he simply wants to be informed. He wants you to produce results that have genuine scientific integrity, whatever they turn out to be. He does not want the fact that he is supporting this endeavor to influence its process or findings in any way."

"That's incredible," said Marty Thomas. "What's the catch? You must admit that it's hard to accept what you're saying at face value!"

"Nevertheless, it is true. The Holy Father has his reasons. I can assure you that your results will be kept as a private communication with Pope John Paul III, and his only condition is that you keep your research secret and do not publish until after his death. We can, in the meantime, take under consideration any measures that you think will assure the credibility of your publication at that itme."

Renee Josephson found herself liking this guy. He was clear, articulate and seemed to have all the angles covered. And he was rather good looking, with an easy manner and a pleasant voice. Tall and dark, too. What the hell was he doing as a priest? Must be gay, she thought.

"Tell us a little about yourself," she said.

"The relevant facts: B.S. Notre Dame, grad school here in Boston, nearly finished a PhD in Physics, but had to make a choice and chose theology over phenomonology. Completed Seminary in Boston, ordained, sent to Rome by the Archbishop to represent him there. I speak science, French, Latin and Spanish and I believe that faith and science can easily co-exist. That's about it."

"Anything more personal?" asked Renee. "Not really. I'm sure we'll get to know each other a bit better over the next weeks...Now if you have no more questions, I'd like to get back to the business at hand. First, you can set aside any concerns about financing your project. I have carte blanche authority to pay for it as we go. It is, in effect, my treat. I am to spare no expense to ensure your success. Be assured, I have ready access to an abundant supply of cash. There will be no problems in that regard. Second, I have already secured most of the supplies and equipment you will require and they are currently being assembled in Turin. If there is any major equipment that was not mentioned in your proposal, or for that matter, any incidental items you might need, let me know and I will procure them. Or you acquire them yourself and I will arrange reimbursement of your costs and their transportation to Italy."

" You see," Paul said with a smile, "why his Holiness chose a priest with a science background to do his bidding!"

The team members could hardly believe what they had just heard. Speaking this time for all of them, Thomas asked again, "What's the catch?" And as before, the answer was: "No catch. Only your committment to quality research and total secrecy."

"Just one more thing," said Paul. Everyone in the room instantly had the same thought: Here it comes...the unacceptable condition.... but before anyone could articulate the thought, McCormack said, "I have tickets here that will take you all to Rome one week from today. I trust that is enough time to get those houses in order!"

CHAPTER 4

I nside Turin Cathederal, it was quiet and the light was dim. It was a peaceful and quite beautiful place. The immense, vaulted space seemed totally unoccupied, but for a small group standing below the shrine of the shroud and looking up to see it, spread open its full length and showing the ghost of an image of a man. The image was not particularly strong or distinct, but it was clearly there. Both his back and front sides were depicted, head to head on the cloth, and there were apparent spots of blood and fluid on his head, side and hands. Marks that brought to mind a whipping covered his back. His hands were crossed over his genital area, and they showed bloody puncture wounds. It was easy to understand why the faithful could believe this to be the burial cloth of Christ. Only one of the investigative team's number had been here before and seen it in person, but no one in the group was in any way surprised by what they saw. It was pretty much what they were prepared for and had expected to see.

The priest who was their escort let his eyes linger on that face. His thoughts unavoidably turned to the life and ministry of the man this cloth was said to portray: The founder of his faith, the Redeemer, the Son of God. The fouder of the Church McCormack served. Could this actually be Him? Was this Jesus? Millions of pilgrims had come here over the course of centuries in the belief that it was. It would certainly be miraculous if it were so; miracles were an article of his Catholic faith, so why couldn't it be so? Could science really resolve the question? Did it really matter, when to merely stand before the reliquary was in itself enough to stimulate a vision of His incredible sacrifice and boundless love? Father Paul whispered a prayer of thanks, crossed himself, and felt ready to get started, his pilgimage of mind and spirit actually at hand.

His little flock of scientists had begun to talk in subdued voices among themselves. It appeared to McCormak that even they felt a sense of deference to this remarkable place. He caught himself about to commit a sin of the mind. He was not superior and they were not infidels; for all he knew, they were all devout Catholics. If His Holiness was correct, a hypothesis that Father Paul was not about to challenge, then they were all here doing God's work. Yes, science and faith could work together. He had been sure of it throughout his life; his life was, he thought, a testament to that belief. Yes, he thought, we're all on the same team - let's get to work.

McCormack led them to a niche in an alcove where they were able to sit and refocus their individual conversations into a single group dialogue. Not surprisingly, the "hard" science folks - John Baptista, Marty Thomas and Renee Josephson - expressed none of spiritual stimulation that the priest felt. Viewing the cloth in person had simply energized their curiosity, and they were peppering each other with a few challenging questions about it. On the other hand, Maria and Matthew were clearly sensitive to the great historical and artistic merits of the Shroud. They were talking softly, at the moment, about provenance and composition. In short order, each of the sub-groups became conscious of the other, and both fell silent. Everyone looked to Dr. Baptista to call them back together as a team.

"OK, folks. The fun is over and now the work begins. Paul, thank you for getting us this far. I'm sure I speak for everyone when I thank you for the brief, but personal tour of Rome, the quick visit to St. Peter's, and especially for that outstanding dinner this evening here in Turin." Everyone nodded concurrent thanks in Father

McCormack's direction. "Getting an initial look at the Shroud and being able to sit here and talk privately in this magnificent cathedral is the icing on the preliminaries. Again, thanks. OK, everybody, let's focus! The main event begins right now."

"By mid-morning tomorrow, the cloth will be in our lab. All of the equipment we've requested is in place and ready for testing. We'll attend to that first; and then we will turn our attention to the Shroud itself. Remember: Our first goal is to determine, to our satisfaction, the authenticity of the shroud. We've all read a great deal of material, mostly produced by a group that last had access to the cloth, that hypothesizes that it is a genuine relic of the resurrection of Jesus Christ. We've also read rebuttals, some apparently based on science, and some not, that suggest research bias, pre-determination of findings, pseudo-science, and outright fabrication. Fortunately, we do not have to judge between these two views, or the credibility of their evidence. We will judge for ourselves, and, in the process, be as certain as it is possible to be of the appropriateness of our methods, the accuracy of our measurements, the integrity of our judgements and the reliability of our findings."

"Questions or comments, so far?" There were none, so he continued...

"The one thing we **can** with some confidence extract from the "literature," such as it is, is a fairly clear and consistent identification of the issues we need to address. Some of them can be resolved with direct scientific evidence. Some will lend themselves more to indirect scientific evidence and informed inference. Some will require our best independent judgement based on historical and artistic knowledge and analysis. It is entirely possible that some questions will defy resolution by any means, but I am pretty certain that in the end we will produce a powerful science-based picture that will point directly to one conclusion or the other."

Marty Thomas spoke up: "Are you done, John? Yes? Well thanks for the literary review and summary of basic research. We all needed that before bedtime..." John took an exaggerated bow and this was greeted with subdued chuckles. "Well, thank you fearless leader. Now," said Marty, "let me take you on a quick tour of the critical questions we want to answer."

"First of all, the image on the shroud. There is no agreement on what it is or how it was made. We need to determine its composition, how it is bonded to the cloth, whether it is anatomically correct, whether it contains any visual clues, and, if possible, to determine how the image was actually created. All of us will play a part in that determination."

"Second, we need to focus on traces of apparent blood and bodily fluids. There is a fundamental disagreement over whether these stains are genuine human biological matter or something else. One "authority" goes so far as to claim that he was able to isolate human blood cells and to type them as AB. On the other hand, the stains have been identified as applied material of some kind. This is a particularly crucial piece of our investigation. We need to make this determination with a considerable degree of certainty. Renee will take the lead on this investigation.

"Third, we need to look at the fabric itself to determine its origin in place and time. This will require both rigorous testing and careful comparisons. That will be up to Maria and me.

"Fourth, we need to consider its history as a relic. How does it compare to the Biblical descriptions of Christ's death, burrial and resurrection? Can we rely on these accounts? What is its documented provenance? Does the face on the cloth appear elsewhere and, if so, when? Does the Church authenticate it as a holy relic? Matthew, that will be your lead."

"Finally, can art and art history add anything to our understanding. It has been suggested by many observers that the shroud is a medieval forgery, an artistic fabrication. Can we challenge or confirm that interpretation? Maria and Matt, you'll work together on this one.

John now reasserted himself: "All of this should give us a pretty good picture on which to base a judgement. Is the Shroud what its champions claim it to be? If so, then we can proceed to phase 2 - our real purpose - can we lift some DNA? If we can, can that DNA tell us anything about the man who was wrapped in that shroud?"

Paul McCormack was stunned. This was definitely NOT in the proposal he had seen. He wondered if it was in the proposal John Paul had seen? He would have to find out. In the meantime, he would follow his instructions to the letter. Enable, do not interfere, report. In the morning, their investigation would begin in earnest.

CHAPTER 5

The lab was well-equipped, relatively spacious, and thoughtfully arranged into at least minimally adequate work areas. John Baptista was both pleased and impressed. Given only a short time to put this in place, Paul McCormack appeared to have achieved another minor miracle. All the essential electronic, chemical, visual and manual tools required for their work stood in place and ready. Most of it looked brand new - which worried John a little bit, because time would have to be spent calibrating, running baselines and what have you and that **could** prove to be a bit of a problem. But this was the kind of problem the team could readily work through so long as all the equipment worked properly. What was the liklihood of that? John knew from more than one personal experience that start-ups rarely went without hiccups of some kind, and no matter how competent and skilled the researcher, one still had to get accustomed to the slightly different operating requirements of one panel or program, one manufacturer, over another. He smiled to himself: He realized that he was beginning to count on those "minor miracles" and was fully expecting a few more along the way. Perhaps the start up would be one of them.

Paul McCormack, standing off to one side, was also pleased. He was confident that he had provided everything the team requested, from some of the most current, expensive and sensitive electronics, right on down to paper, pencils and a coffee maker. It had been difficult, but not impossible, to procure all this "stuff" in the short time he had had to do it. Fortunately, much-needed assistance had come from the small scientific community at the Vatican. They had done well. The logistics involved in assembling all this material at the Cathedral complex, and the need to avoid arousing unwanted outside interest had proven difficult but manageable. The really "impossible" task was installation. He used contractors to move things into this very private space, other contractors to set everything up, and a few highly-skilled people to test and calibrate the technical tools. They had finished up only last night, while he, himself, and the team were paying their respects to the shroud. It **was** a minor miracle and he felt real pleasure at being able to turn a working lab over to Dr. Baptista this morning, right on schedule.

John and Paul chatted for a few minutes about the lab, and when he was made aware of the pre-testing and calibration that had already been done, Baptista was not entirely surprised. The miracle **he** had half expected was, in fact, confirmed. Neither one of them thought much, if at all, about the coincidence between their names and that of the Pope, and if they had both of them would have taken it at face value - a curious coincidence. Nonetheless, with all the "minor miracles" that seemed to be associated with this adventure, one or the other of them might have had cause to wonder. But wonder they did not. Instead, they got to work.

The entire team was in the lab, now, busily familiarizing themselves with their resources. The scientists among them, John, Martin and Renee, were conducting various test runs and getting comfortable with their technical equipment. Maria and Matt were seated in a corner of the lab examining a large archive of research and historical data, establishing their on-line data bases, and glancing, from time to time, at the object of their inquiry, laid out full length under special lighting on a table at the center of the room. Paul McCormack stood silently at the head of the table as if on guard, but actually in quiet contemplation. He simply could not move his eyes - or his mind - from that haunting face on the shroud. But for Paul, no one had actually yet approached the cloth, let alone touched it. Maria and Matt looked at each other, stood up in tandem and made their way to the table.

Last night they had looked up to view the shroud from a distance, inside its sealed case hung fairly high on the Cathedral wall. It had been possible to take it all in in a single view, to see it as a whole and complete object. It had not looked to Maria, then, as large as it actually was here on the table. This reminded her that perception could be a tricky thing. Judgements made in isolation of context could be made by science, but the context might confirm or confound the scientific finding. Maria wasn't concerned about investigator bias. That constituted outright human error and resulted in bad science. She was thinking more, in her mind, of good research, where the facts of science and the accurate perceptions of informed observation complement each other and create a tightly-woven web of probability.

Maria circled the shroud slowly. Her trained eye was engaged in an initial broad search for any anomolies in the image: Things that might be obvious to the specially trained artistic eye which would probably be overlooked by the average observer; things that might set off what she thought of as her internal authenticity alarm. As she moved around the table, she started to pick things out and catalogue them in her mind. This was really exciting, but she also found herself feeling a sense of disappointment as she completed her circuit. This was too easy. There were so many problems. She would certainly examine them all more closely - intensely if necessary - but without even considering the weave of the fabric, she had to wonder how any neutral observer could conclude this cloth was authentic. Her immediate visceral reaction was that John would be disappointed. Be that as it may, Maria was almost convinced. She believed that art objects spoke to her, and her first conversation with the shroud told her there was nothing miraculous here.

While Maria circumnavigated the table, Matt stood, still and silent, to one side. His look at the cloth was limited to a more casual scan. From his perspective as antiquarian and historian, there was no doubt that this was the authentic Shroud of Turin. Confirmation for the record. Done. But what, precisely, was he authenticating? A piece of cloth, the image of a man, the burn marks and lead stains from a 16th century fire (from which, incidentally, the cloth had almost miraculously survived destruction). Yes, this was the true relic that had been venerated for so long by so many, but was the relic true? Not very likely, he thought. The confirmable provenance of **this** shroud only extended to the 11th century. At that time, and throughout the later middle ages, it was only one of many on display around Christiandom. Too bad none of the others are known to have survived. He would love to compare the image on this shroud to at least a couple of others. But, as far as he knew, there were not only no other survivors, but no pictures of any of them, either. He made a mental note to undertake a more extensive search. But provenance was not what was really troubling. After all, lots of genuine historical artifacts had spotty, or even totally lacking provenance. What really bothered him was that the image was just too perfect in its detailed portrayal of a crucified man...exactly as described in the Bible. In his experience, most relics that so perfectly conformed to expectation were fake. Of course, that didn't mean, necessarily, that the Shroud of Turin was fake, but it certainly cast a broad shadow on Matt's thinking.

Back in their corner, Matt and Maria sipped coffee and shared their initial perceptions. They talked through the work they planned to do over the next few days and about how much of it was complimentary research. Coordination would make it go both more quickly and more easily. Perhaps, in the end, they could jointly deliver a single, integrated set of findings...assuming, of course, that that's the way things actually turned out. However remote, there was always a chance....

CHAPTER 6

L ate evening, back at the hotel. The six of them were seated at a large, round dining table, the remains of dessert and coffee still not cleared. At this hour, they were the only patrons in the place and they were in no hurry to leave. It had been a long, hard, intense workday, one without a break for lunch. In fact, they has worked well into the evening hours and stopped only when hunger and fatigue demanded it. As enabler in chief, Paul had offered to go to the hotel dining room and order for all of them so the resarchers would have a chance to freshen up before they ate. None of them was much interested, at this point, in ordering from the menu - or even looking at it - so they left it to Paul to decide and headed for their rooms. All of them except Renee. She liked this priest. He was pleasant, competent, real; and she was curious about why he had chosen the church over the laboratory. For his part, he found himself attracted to Renee's professional competence and personal elegance. He wanted to know more about her, too. So he was pleased when she stayed behind and accompanied him into the dining room. They put their heads together and decided to order 2 meat entrees, 2 chicken entrees, 2 fish entrees and salad all around. A tray of local meats and cheeses would serve as the appetizer (as if they really needed one!), and they rounded out their order with bottles of red, white and rose wine. They decided to leave the dessert selection to each diner's discretion. Order placed, they sat at the table and shared drinks and small talk.

When the other members of the group returned, they found Paul and Renee nibbling on the appetizers, the wine bottles open on the table, and the entrees about to be served. They had a bit of fun determining who would get what to eat, but everyone was happy with the selections Paul and Renee had made, and they got down to the business of eating. There was little conversation as they ate; they were tired and hungry and needed to re-fuel. Dinner over, dessert and coffee re-energized them, and they began to chat among themseleves. John Baptista was reluctant to bring an untimely end to the pleasantries, but he was the boss and he had to do it. He tapped his glass gently with his teaspoon and, when he had everyone's attention, he said, "OK, folks, let's take a few minutes before we hit the hay to debrief the day and talk a little about tomorrow." Someone sighed, they all chuckled, then pulled themselves together and focused their attention on John.

"Let me begin by telling you what I've been doing. We - myself and Marty - started the day checking the instrument callibrations and running a few trials to familiarize ourselves with their operation. Everything checks out. We spent some time, with Renee, examining the image on the cloth. Renee can tell you what **she** was looking for. I was looking for potential sources of dna. Marty was intrigued with the image itself. By this evening, I had found a couple of concentrations of apparent blood and body fluids that might lend themselves to an extraction, assuming that these concentrations are, in fact, biological reminants. Tomorrow we'll have to make some decisions about if, when and how to capture a sufficient amount of this material for dna sampling. Since the "if" depends heavily upon your findings, Renee, why don't you tell us where you are?"

Renee hesitated for a moment, reflecting on her day, then said, "Well, John, I have been doing a very careful visual review of all the apparent staining on the body image. Frankly, I'm not immediately convinced that any of it is actually biological...or at least not human.

I am not prepared to go into all the reasons that raise doubts, but let me make note of two things: The "blood" stains appear, to the naked eye and under low magnification, to be something other than human blood. Perhaps a pigment of some kind, perhaps animal in origin. I don't want to make too much of this just yet, because, as we all know only too well, the eye can mislead. There is, however, another concern. If any of this particular staining was actually left by fresh human blood, one would expect some evidence of leak-through staining on the back side of the cloth and that appears to be lacking. Now it is always possible that leak through would not, for a variety of reasons, take place, and I have not thoroughly examined the back side of every stain, so for the moment I want to refrain from making any serious judgement. We'll know a lot more after tomorrow." As she finished up, she caught herself sneaking a peek at Paul to see if he posited any reaction. None that she could discern. She was aware that she felt a sense of relief; he was not upset with her findings. That's a good thing, she thought...

Dr. Thomas, meanwhile, was reporting that he was puzzled by the image of the man. It was like nothing he had ever seen in the world of radiology. As described over and over again in the literature, it was entirely superficial to the cloth - no penetration at all into the weave. It showed three dimensional depth, but no distortion in areas that would have curved around the head and body had a dead person been wrapped in this cloth. It had some of the characteistics of a sonogram, some of the characteristics of an x-ray and some of the characteristics of a photogaphic negative. "Hard to figure," Marty concluded. "I'm going to run some analyses in the morning, if I can get some sample material."

"OK, Marty," said John. "We'll have to see what kind of sampling we can do given the non-destructive mandate. Perhaps we can discuss this more with you tomorrow, Paul?"

"I look forward to the conversation."

"Thanks, Paul. Now, Maria, what have you and Matt got for us?"

"Well, we did a pretty thorough visual exam, too Without going into too much detail, I found a number of suspicious anamolies in the image. I've begun to look more carefully at each of them and I expect to know a lot more by this time tomorrow. I also took some super-high resolution photos of the fabric weave and I'm in the process of running them through multiple data banks for comparisons. I'll let you all know what I find as quickly as I can. How about you, Matt?"

"Not a lot to add," said Matt. "I can confirm that the Shroud is the authentic relic we came to study. I suppose that's important, but it's also pretty obvious. Like the others, I've found several areas of concern - the iconography for one, the provenance for another - but I'm not ready to close the book. Far from it - the concerns are the open door to further investigation, and that's what I'll be about bright and early..."

"Sounds like a great plan for all of us," said John. Let's knock off and get some rest!"

CHAPTER 7

Day two in the lab. Paul McCormack, John Baptista and Renee Josephson were discussing something that seemed simple, but really wasn't simple at all. Something that could have a dramatic impact on the science they could do and the viability of their findings. Something that could damage what had so far been an outstanding relationship between McCormack and the research team. That simple something, simply stated, was how to define "non-destructive." Renee wanted a sample of the "blood" sufficient for several chemical analyses. To get the sample, she had presented three options. Each had positive and negative implications for both the cloth and the research. Scraping some of the desired material from the surface of the shroud would, if done with care and expertise, do little or no damage to the fabric but would, of course, arguably remove and destroy something that had presumably been part of the relic from its origin. The analytical problem with this method was the possibility that the material left on the surface had been separated and was clinically different from material that might have been absorbed into the fabric before the liquid had dried. A second method proposed by Renee was to saturate a small area of the stain with liquid emulsifier, then vacuum the liquid up for analysis. This would capture any absorbed material, but it ran the risk of permanently staining the fabric. In addition, it would, of course, permanently remove some original material. Finally, they could remove a small piece of stained cloth and conduct their anayses with confidence that they had what would normally be considered a scientifically acceptable sample. This would clearly be destructive not only of the stain, but of the fabric itself. From the point of view of preservation, this was the least acceptable option.

Renee argued that pieces of the cloth had been cut and used for scientific testing in the past, but Paul countered that these pieces were taken from an outer edge and had no impact on the appearance of the relic to casual observers. Cutting a piece out of the image? Unthinkable. Their slightly raised voices and Renee's tone of evident frustration caught Martin's attention from where he was setting up a piece of equipment. He joined the discussion.

"Maybe we don't really need to take a physical sample," he offered. We can rig up a system to look at the stains in situ using high-powered magnification. For that matter, we can bounce some light off them and get a pretty clear chemical analysis."

John wanted to agree and bring an end - and a solution - to the disagreement. But for reasons of his own, he couldn't do that. The time might come when **he** would require a significant physical sample to conclude his part in the research, so he had to leave that option on the table. Meanwhile, Renee was continuing to object, saying that Tom's solution was fine, as far as it went, but that she could certainly extract more and better information from a prepared sample. Her lab was all set, and it would certainly weaken the validity of their ultimate findings if she were unable to run her tests.

In the end, it was Paul who provided a short-term but workable solution that was completely satisfactory to none of them, but sufficient to keep the research moving along.

"Look," he said. "Perhaps there will never be a need to destroy anything. Maybe we can just put this discussion off to another day. Renee, I will authorize you to take some scrapings for your chemical analyses. Marty can conduct his tests in situ. Then we can look at the results and see where they lead us. If they are conclusive in one way or another, fine. If not, and additional sampling could reasonably be expected to resolve the issue, then we can re-visit this conversation. Remember, I'm not here to throw up roadblocks. My job is to enable your work, and enable it I will, even if that means bending the rules a bit to get a final answer."

That is, if we ever get close enough to an answer for rule-bending to be justified, he thought.

Renee was not really happy with Paul's solution, but it was the best offer she had heard today - the only offer, really - so she reluctantly signed on. Made sense, really: let's see where this thing goes and only go ten rounds if we have to.

Dr. Thomas was well-pleased with his contribution and was just about ready to carry out the tests he had proposed. He went back to his work area and continued his preparations.

John was happy, too. His team had successfully worked through a tough issue with their Vatican emissary. Everyone had maintained their professional bearing, their work could continue, and Paul had committed to at least keeping open the question of removing material from the shroud. And it struck him for the first time that Father McCormack was not just their enabler. He was their friend. He, and presumably the man he represented, Pope John Paul III, wanted them to succeed. They had told him that, and now, for the first time, he truly believed it. There was no hidden agenda here after all. John was now sure that, in the end, if the oportunity presented itself, he would be permitted to do whatever had to be done.

Over in their corner, Matt and Maria paid little attention to the activities across the room. It was late afternoon and they were already working on the outline of a preliminary report. They had spent the last few hours reviewing what they thought they knew, challenging each other's views, crystalizing their thinking. There were still a few open questions, but, for the most part, they were satisfied with their findings. They were consistent with the most credible known data, with their own knowledge of art, history and historical relics, and, collectively, formed a coherent answer to the question of the Shroud's authenticity. The hard sciences might find what they may, but Matt and Maria had little doubt that what the others discovered would almost certainly corroborate their own findings.

First, the image of the man. They were not yet able to venture a likely hypothesis as to how the image was made, or who might have made it, but they were convinced that it was, with a very high degree of certainty, man made. The image presented too many problems to be anything other than a deliberate medieval forgery, intended to decieve. And they were pretty sure that the forger was not concerned about what the 21st century would think of his work; he was more interested in producing a for-profit holy relic - one for the trade, as it were. Or perhaps he was a devout Christian, whose portrait of Christ in all his suffering, was intended to draw pilgrims and inspire belief. The who and why were, of course, speculation. But the rest, even the speculation itself, on reflection, was well-grounded on a long list of additional evidence and supporting facts.

Fact: The image of the front of the man is significantly shorter than the image of his back. There was no possible natural explanation for this, but it would be perfectly normal for an artistic creation.

Fact: The man's eyes are covered with coins. This was not at any time a Jewish practice or tradition. Rather, it was a Western European tradition based on the Greek myth of paying a ferryman to cross the River Styx. Jesus and his contemporaries would likely not have known about this practice, and, if they did, would almost certainly not have adopted it. On the other hand, this was a common practice in the Middle Ages.

Fact: Jewish burrial practice at the time of Jesus called for **wrapping** a **washed** body in a shroud. It would have been remarkable to have entombed Jesus's body unwashed. It was equally unlikely that they would simply have draped him head to toe. Two highly unlikelies make one fairly strong probably not.

Fact: If the body had actually been covered head to toe, any 3 dimensional image projected from that body - a totally unsubstantiated hypothesis in itself- would have been significantly distorted. There is no distortion of that kind on the Shroud.

Fact: The face of the man on the cloth is clearly intended to be Jesus. The face on the shroud is a derivation of 800 years of Christian tradition, consistent with a depiction traceable not to the holy land, but to Constantinople.

Fact: For the first several hundred years, Jesus was depicted as a beardless man. This image appears on many early Christian tombs and meeting places, including some in Rome. If we assume that Peter lived and died in Rome, and that Peter knew Jesus in life, then why didn't Peter correct this error?

Fact: The various bloody marks on the shroud run along the image in the same general north to south pattern - the pattern we would expect to see on a statue of Jesus hanging on the cross, but not what we would expect to see on a prone figure.

Fact: The various wound and scourge marks appear to be entirely superficial - they do not bleed through to the other side of the cloth. The implication is that they have been applied to enhance the appearance of the image.

Fact: The overall image is entirely consistent with other medieval images of Jesus and the shroud is one of more than 30 that are reported in the literature to have existed in the 12th to 15th centuries. There is absolutely **no** evidence that this shroud existed prior to the other 30 or that they were copied from it.

Fact: The overall image is consistent with other images of Jesus that can be definitively attributed to a date earlier than the one to which we can confidently attribute the shroud.

Fact: The Bible speaks of a Suderium, or face cloth, which would have covered Jesus' face. That cloth should have absorbed most of the blood and fluids leaking from a dead body. The various blood marks on the shroud face show no diminishing or distortion that might be attributed to an intervening piece of linen.

Fact: The weave of the cloth is entirely consistent with Western European manufacture in the 12th century. There is absolutely no basis for suggesting that this cloth was woven in the Middle East a thousand years earlier.

Fact: Other medieval renditions of the crucified Christ show nails in his wrists. That was not the common placement of the spikes, but it did appear in statuary from time time, notably in the region of France where the shroud made its first appearance. Perhaps this was a local artistic tradition. In any case, several of these depictions pre-date the arrival of the shroud by nearly 100 years.

One Final Fact: Over the centuries, the Vatican has proclaimed that hundreds of Christian relics are genuine and worthy of veneration. Yet the Schroud of Turin, arguably the **ultimate** relic of Christ, has never received such an endorsement. The public position of the Church is that it is an object of "faith and belief," and it is up to the individual worshiper to decide for him or herself if they are looking at "The Real Jesus."

———

Maria and Matt reviewed their Facts. They had reached a conclusion. From their collective point of view, and in each of their independent professional judgements, the case was compelling, if not absolutely conclusive. It was highly likely - should they say "probable" - that the shroud was a fake. They did not know exactly how it was made. There was speculation in the literature that a camera obscura produced the image. The distance of the figure - man or statue - from the camera would account nicely for the difference in front and back images: The distance between camera and object was different for the two images. Nice theory. Perhaps there would be traces of urine, used to sensitize the cloth consistent with this theory, that could be discovered by chemical analysis. They would have to bring that possibility to Renee's attention. There was also a question of the presence or absence of annointing oils, herbs and spices, which were a traditional part of 1st century Jewish funerary practice. Maria and Matt had seen no evidence of the presence of these things, but that didn't mean they weren't there. To be thorough, they should bring this to Renee's attention, as well. But those were really the only potential loose ends.

They decided to pass those loose ends along to Renee, but to keep the rest of their findings under wraps for the moment. They did not want to influence the scientific investigation in any way. John, Martin and Renee could and would reach their own conclusions. Matt and Maria were pretty sure they already knew what those conclusions would be...

CHAPTER 8

By the middle of the third day in the lab, John Baptista, the **scientist**, had become convinced that there would be no need to revisit the discussion about destructive gathering of samples. John Baptista, the **man**, was disappointed. The evidence was leading away from where he wished it would take them. In fact, his team was building a **wall** of evidence that supported the negative hypothesis. The Shroud could not be the burial cloth of Christ, ergo, it could not yield the precious biological cargo he was after. The latest blow to his hopes had come just minutes ago, when Renee and Marty had come to him with a preliminary report of their findings. The data was clear: There was no human biological material in the samples Renee had taken the day before. Period. Yes, there were some elements of blood detected, but these had been detected by previous researchers and attributed to a pigment used by medieval artists in yellow, orange and red paint. Shroud enthusiasts had questioned this attribution and insisted that the finding actually proved the presence of blood. Not so, according to Renee and Martin. They had shared their lab results with Maria and she had confirmed the artistic use of such pigments. Since there were no other elements present in the sample, and the professional judgement of an independent art expert supported their conclusion, that was it: No Blood.

John was far from devastated, but he was deflated. "What the hell," he thought, "Am I Don Quixote?" It was time to get down off the horse and deal with the facts. He called the team together to assess what to do next. His immediate thought was, "Let's shut it down and get back to our real lives..." But that's not what he would say. He would let them decide...

Paul McCormack had spent a good part of the day with Maria and Matt, talking about their draft report, so, as they joined the others, he had a pretty good idea why the impromptu meeting had been called. Not good news for True Believers, he thought...and not good news for John, either. He realized he was pulling for John, was hoping he would succeed, but not to prove the True Believers were right. Paul really didn't care about that. Whether the Shroud was real or fake made not a jot of difference in his faith or his life. And John Paul had been clear: Enable them, wherever it leads. No, he, like John, had been hoping that the Shroud would lead them to a glimpse of the **real** Jesus - not a face on a cloth, but the real, biological human being...

John shared the clinical results briefly and without comment. There was no blood. He summarized Maria and Matt's expert analysis. Inauthentic. "OK, folks," he said, "Where do we go from here?"

He fully expected someone to say, "Home." But instead of throwing in the towel, Renee tossed up an intriguing idea. "Maybe," she said, "the 'blood' is an artistic enhancement. Maybe there's still a little bit of wiggle room in the historical analysis. We still don't know with any certainty how the image was made. Let's suppose for a moment that it is, somehow, genuine. Let's suppose that alleged errors in the carbon dating process are real and that the cloth actually is 1st century. Let's suppose that the man in the shroud is Jesus and that his body was washed before it was wrapped. The image would then necessarily lack all the telltale blood marks that "prove" it is Christ to the pilgrim who views it. Suppose the **blood** was added, but the **fluid** stains were not. Suppose **they** are real. None of this is likely, but it is possible, so maybe we should evaluate a sample of that fluid."

"What the hell," interjected Martin, "We're here, we're all set up. Let's give it a shot."

Matt spoke up. "Wait a minute, wait a minute! The only serious question still out there is how the image was made. If we're going to do any more clinical testing, why not focus on that?"

John responded immediately. "I can think of several reasons. First of all, based on the failure of 100 years of study to answer that question, it will be a tough nut to crack. We don't even know where to begin, nor do we have reason to believe that we might succeed where so many others have failed. We'd have to prove that a miracle happened at the time of Christ's resurrection and that it was captured on cloth. I just don't see that as a fruitful investigation. And even if we were to somehow succeed, that success brings us no closer to useful biologicals. No, let's leave the creation of the image to speculation for the time being...."

Paul inquired, "What kind of sample would be needed, Renne?"

"Liquefaction and suction, Paul. We talked about it yesterday. Might pose a risk to the appearance of the cloth, I'm not sure. The emulsifier could react with whatever material is on the cloth and leave a stain..."

Paul looked to John. "What do you think? Is it worth the risk? Could it give you what you need?

"Not likely, Paul, but I suppose it's within the range of the possible. The alternative is that we pack up and go home, so if you're willing to take the risk, perhaps we could give it a try..."

Paul thought about his instructions and he thought about the Pope's expectations. These were people of integrity and good conscious, and who knows where it would lead..."Let's give it a try," he said.

Renee dropped a microscopic amount of the chemical onto one of the "fluid" stains and watched, on her screen, for signs of staining. None. Encouraged, she next used half a cc of the liquid. Still no signs of staining, but there were signs that the some of the "fluid" was lifting from the cloth. Not all of it, she hoped, because that would produce a visible loss of material. To her relief, the background fluid coloration remained intact.

Paul was watching her carefully. She shared the results with him. He looked over to John, then said, "Okay, Renee, let's go for it."

As it turned out, their fears for the safety of the cloth and its visual integrity were unfounded. Renee was able to lift enough of the fluid material to conduct her testing, and no apparent evidence of the vacuuming was left behind.

Renee and Tom got to work adjusting equipment, preparing the sample, running the tests. It was only a matter of minutes before the initial results were in: Yes, this was biological material! No time for celebrations. No celebrations were in order. This was scientific research, and the next step was to isolate the biologics and try to determine exactly what they were.

Another twenty minutes. Then, "Albumin. Egg white." Renee shook her head. She knew what Maria was about to say.

"That about shuts the door," proclaimed their art expert friend. "Albumin was a staple part of a medieval artist's kit. It was used as a bonding agent with pigments. Evidentally, it was used on the Shroud to simulate the fluid stains. No real use to us, but more evidence that the Shroud was concocted by some pretty smart and talented people back in the 12th century."

———

John Baptista again felt that pang of disappointment, made worse this time by the fact that his own wife had delivered the fatal blow. How could she? Because it was true, of course. God, he loved that woman! The opening line of one of John's favorite poems popped into his mind: The time has come, the walrus said... yes, they'd eaten up all their options. Nothing left now but to digest the disappointment and get on home. He called everyone together...

Before John could say a word, Matthew Hightower spoke up. "You know," he said, "I've been thinking and perhaps there's another option. We've all been focused on the shroud, and rightly so. But, you know, the shroud has a sort of cousin, called the Sudarium. It has a documented history to a very early date and it has been associated with Jesus from the beginning...."

Maria joined in: "Yes, Matt, I read about it in our research. It's supposed to be the cloth that covered Christ's face when he was taken from the cross. Can you tell us a bit more?"

"Sure. It's definitely a relic from the early days of Christianity. It's a small cloth, the size of a hand towel, and is unquestionably of 2000 year old Middle Eastern weave. It bears no image, just blood and fluid stains. It has a documented history of travel going back at least 1800 years. We know it originated in Palestine, came from the middle east, through North Africa and on to medieval Spain, all in a long-term and ultimately successful effort to keep it out of Muslim hands. It has been an object of pilgrimage and veneration in Valencia Cathedral for almost 1000 years. Shroud enthusiasts have tried to link it to the Turin image, but, at least in my mind, not very convincingly. I think it stands alone. And maybe, just maybe, it's the real thing..."

John Baptista mentally kicked himself in the butt. Why hadn't he known about this thing? Paul McCormack realized that he'd known most of this all along, but never made the connection to what they were about here in Turin. Renee Josephson exclaimed, "Jesus! Maybe we've been looking in the wrong place!" Marty Thomas was sceptical. At least the shroud had the image of the man they were looking for. If they had found biologicals, they could at least claim they were connected to Jesus. But this new thing they were talking about? "It's a shot in the dark," he said.

Perhaps our last shot, thought John. Perhaps...

CHAPTER 9

V alencia Cathederal. Only the three hard science folks, along with Paul McCormack, had made the flight to Spain. Maria and Matt were left behind to do more research on the provenance of the Suderium. Paul had connected them with an archivist at the Vatican, and they were now in Rome searching for information. They would have all the help they required. In fact, John, Martin and Renee would also have all the help they needed here in Valencia. Paul had called the Papal Secretary from Turin to update His Holiness and ask for guidance. The response had been almost immediate: The team was authorized limited access to the Suderium - limited only, in fact, by Father McCormack's best judgement. The Office of the Holy Father would notify the Archbishop in Valencia that the scientists were there not only with the Pope's permission, but at his direction and with his blessing. The Archbishop would know how to respond. Consequently, he personally welcomed them, delivering the reliquary case holding the Suderium into their hands, and offering to make himself available on call should they need his guidance or assistance in any way. He handed them the key to the ornate, medieval case and left them to their work.

They brought the case to a small, secure, private chapel adjoining the main building. Here they opened the reliquary and saw the Suderium for the first time. It was carefully folded into a square shape and showed immediate evidence of random marks and stains. With gloved hands, they removed the cloth and laid it carefully on a prepared surface. Now they could see that the random marks were part of a larger pattern. There was nothing vague about the pattern. It was strong and clear, and, to the naked eye, the staining appeared ancient and genuine. It took them a few minutes to get oriented to the pattern, but when they did, its meaning was clear. This cloth had apparently been wrapped around the face of a dead man, and the staining reflected a series of small, bloody wounds to the forehead and a considerable amount of expulsed bronchial fluid around the nose and mouth. The stains followed the rounded contours of a three dimensional face, and appeared to flow the way they should. There was, of course, no face - just the tracings of fluid left behind in a discernable pattern on the cloth. Most of the stains penetrated all the way through the cloth; a few, the lighter ones, had not. This reinforced their sense that this cloth might indeed be the real thing. Certainly it was worth the testing they planned to do. They got right to work.

It was essential not to damage this cloth in any visible way. Renee placed the cloth under her portable microscope. She put a pinpoint droplet of blood reagent on one of the red stains and watched carefully. The reaction, tiny but clear, was almost immediate. It told her that this stain might be human blood. She stood back and let the others take a look. Silent head nodding. So far, so good. She repeated the process with a miniscule drop of reagent and the result was the same. She motioned over for Paul to take a look. He did, and understood her unspoken question. God's on our side, he thought. Go for it, Rennee. He nodded to her and she dropped a full cc of emulsifier on the blood stain. The stain liquified, but left most of the ancient blood discoloration on the cloth. This looked really promising, and there was no associated chemical discoloring. Again, she showed Paul first, and then the others.

"OK. This looks good," said John. "If it's okay with you, Paul, lets take some samples."

Paul spoke first to Renee: "Nice work, Renee." He smiled faintly in her direction and then turned to John. "Let's do it" was all he said.

Late that evening, back at the lab in Turin, they were anxious to analyze their samples. They had taken more than a dozen in the course of the day, half blood and half fluid. Not only did they have multiple samples, they had also harvested a considerable amount of material. They had more than enough to run their tests, enough for several trial runs if that proved necessary. In the event, they only needed to run the analysis of each kind of sample twice: Once to identify it and a second time to validate the initial results. Renee and Martin carefully managed the samples, controlled the chemical and electronic processes, and interpreted the results. After the first test runs, Marty called out 'BINGO! We have human blood and human saliva!" The second run of testing confirmed this amazing result.

The next step was to determine how degraded this ancient material might be. They did not have the equipment in their temporary lab to make that determination, and John was loathe to do it himself, anyway. He certainly had the necessary skills, and if this determination wasn't so important and he was working with his own equipment in his own lab, he might have taken it on. But the additional analysis **was** critical, and he wasn't home, so he found it both necessary and desirable to defer to a lab that specialized in dna identification and extraction. It was, in any case, the correct option because it would result in a totally idependent blind analysis. Fortunately, there were a number of these labs in Europe; they had popped up all over the place as dna research and application grew into big business. They were, generally speaking, quite reliable if you were able to pay their sometimes substantial fees. John and Paul did an informed internet search, and quickly came to agreement on a well-respected lab, suitably located in Rome. Paul called them and was pleased to discover it was a 24 hour operation; he made arrangements to meet with them at their facility the next day. Marty and Renee shut down the equipment, stored the samples, and flopped into their chairs quite exhausted.

All of a sudden, it was dead quiet in the lab and there was nothing more to do. They sat, absorbed in their own thoughts, not speaking, for quite awhile. Then Dr. Thomas said, "Just one problem, folks - how in the hell do we know **whose** dna we're in the process of capturing?" That, of course, was now the million dollar question, but no one was ready to consider it even fleetingly tonight. "We're all spent," said John. "It may not even matter. Let's wait and see what the dna people can give us. Why don't we all drag ourselves back to the hotel, have a night cap, and get some sleep…"

The next day, the entire team assembled over lunch at a charming little restaurant that they had been fortunate enough to discover just down the street from the dna lab. John had called Maria late the previous night to share an abbreviated version of the visit to Valencia and their success in extracting blood and saliva samples. He had arranged to meet Matt and Maria at the lab at noon. Father McCormack had taken the lead in a brief meeting with the facility director. He told the man only that he represented the Vatican, that he had samples that required immediate analysis, that cost was not an issue, and that what he wanted was to determine the presence and viability of any dna contained in those samples. A result by the end of the day would be quite acceptable; tomorrow mid-day at the latest. The director assured Paul that this would not be a problem, and McCormack then took care of all the required paperwork. Lastly, he paid the fee, shook hands with the director, returned to the team, which awaited him in the lobby, and led them down the street for lunch.

While they ate, Matt and Maria recounted how their day of research had gone. "In a word," said Maria, "Swimmingly!" They had concentrated their efforts on finding early references to the Sudarium and they had found them aplenty in the Vatican Archives. The earliest records were Roman Imperial, early fourth century. They contained a clear description of the Sudarium, along with several other artifacts viewed by Emperess (later Saint) Helena, the Emperor Constantine's mother. She had made the long journey to the Holy Land in search of true relics of Christ. She brought many of them back to Rome, where some still reside in the Vatican Museums. Others, including the Sudarium, already had permanent homes in Jerusulem in the care of the Early Church. Helena believed that the Sudarium had been taken from the tomb of Jesus by Mary (it is uncertain whether the reference was to Jesus' mother or to Mary Magdalene), had been carefully preserved and handed down in an unbroken line from the apostles, to the deacons and finally to the Bishops of the Church. From then on, its existence was referenced several times over the centuries, and its travels - for travel it did - are well-documented. It ended up in Spain, just ahead of the Moors, in the 8th century and found a permanent home in Valencia. It was enshrined by King Alfonso II in 840, in a purpose-built chapel that later became the Cathederal. It has remained in the possession of the Bishops and been housed in the Cathedral ever since. It's a small cloth, not much bigger than a handkerchief, and it has been preserved in a silver-covered shrine since it was placed there in 1075 by Alfons VI.

"We can't say for certain that the Suderium covered Christ's face," Maria summarized, " but both of us have concluded that the association of the Sudarium with Jesus has a firm foundation in historical tradition and a verifiable provenance dating back almost to the time of Christ."

CHAPTER 10

They were gathered in the hotel dining room sharing a continental breakfast. Maria thought how much better this was - the real thing - than even the better ones that had been served at Museum functions back home. She locked in for just a moment on the words "back home." This had been a fantastic week in Europe, an amazing, once in a lifetime adventure. It was almost as if she'd been transported back to her days of graduate school, when she traveled the continent to see and study first-hand the great works of Western art. A few exciting days with no staff meetings, no 9 to 5 and most definitely no routine. It had been genuine fun and the team had worked so well together. She was quite pleased for John that he had found what he was looking for, even if it turned out to be hiding in an unexpected place. Now, if only they can isolate some dna...her thoughts flipped back to home... home and John. When they got home, perhaps, just perhaps they could make that baby they so desperately wanted...yes, she thought, it's been fun but it's time to go home.

For his part, John was suffering from a slowly-building, gradually intensifying anxiety. They had not heard from the lab by late last night, and there were no calls so far this morning. If there was no dna all the planning, expense, inconvenience and hard work that had gone into this expedition would be in vain. Not hearing was probably a good thing, he told himself. They found something and they're working on extraction and duplication. Gotta be. But, deep down, he was not really reassured; the anxiety was still there. He had never been especially good at handling his nerves, but this was downright maddening. He tried eating a croissant and washed it down with coffee. Ugh, that was a mistake; didn't help at all...

Renee and Marty were having a perfectly unemotional scientific conversation about the likelihood that recoverable dna was actually present in their samples. They knew that dna survival in ancient remains was dependent partly on the nature of the artifact, partly on conditions of preservation, and partly on pure chance. It has been well-preserved, for example, in frozen mammoth tissue; so well-preserved that recovered and replicated mammoth dna has prompted a scientific conversation about the possibility of cloning one. Ancient Human dna is most often successfully extracted from undamaged teeth. The enamel acts much like a bottle or can, to preserve its contents. Bone is a secondary source, but most of the time bone is too degraded - decayed, fossilized or otherwise environmentally changed - to be useful. Blood and fluid dna is used every day in medical facilities and criminal investigations. It is commonplace, relatively simple - a mouth swab can provide all the sample needed - and technically reliable. Anybody who is familiar with criminal forensics knows how blood and fluids are used to provide unique dna identifiers and catch the crook. But what were the chances of getting anything useful from **ancient** blood and fluids? "I have no idea, really," concluded Renee. "Maybe John has some idea; maybe we should do a little research after breakfast?" Dr. Thomas, ever the sceptic, replied, "My guess is, not likely; but why waste time on research. We'll hear from the lab soon enough, so let's enjoy the food..."

Matt and Paul were chatting, too. Matt was describing some of the most famous Christian relics, pieces of the True Cross, the wooden "King of the Jews" tablet, crucifiction nails, blood, fingers, bones, all manner of otherwise grotesque souvenirs. There were enough pieces of the "True" Cross out there to build a house - a house held together by an abundance of those nails ; enough Holy Foreskins for an army of men. (To his knowledge, no one had ever claimed to possess Jesus' stool. Matt chuckled to himself: If some turned up, that would certainly give new meaning to the exclamation, "Holy Crap!"). Back on point, at least some of these relics were probably genuine, most were not. But it didn't really matter. At its core, all religion is founded on belief, not fact. The relics of Christianity, preserved or manufactured, have been objects of veneration precisely because they are representatives of belief. Veneration of these objects has driven pilgrimages and even crusades because they bring the believer into real physical contact with those beliefs. They are proof that the belief is true, they open a door between the supplicant and God, they are miraculous. "Yes," Paul agreed, pensively. "I agree - whether they're genuine or not only matters to scientists and historians. Holy relics **are** really all about belief..."

They were just standing to leave when Paul's phone rang. He looked at the caller i.d. and held up a finger for everyone to stay put. He put the phone to his ear and carried on a brief conversation in Italian. He hung up. His face betrayed nothing. He let the tension mount for just a moment, then smiled. "They've done it," he said.

There was a collective exhalation of held breath and a second or two of silence. Then John asked, "What exactly have they done, Paul?"

"They've extracted the dna of a single individual. Not pieces, but the whole thing. And they've had absolutely no trouble in replicating it. They want to know what we want to do next: Pick up the samples and products, or let them interpret the dna?"

"No question about that, Paul," responded John. "Let them do the interpretation."

John hoped that they could infer some significant information about the person who provided that dna so long ago. At the very least, confirm sex and place of origin. Perhaps a bit more. He also realized that all the results would have to be confirmed by at least two other independent labs. And when they got back to Boston, he would run the same protocols in his own lab...just to satisfy himself, once and for all. But that was in the future. For the time being it would be enough to get as much additional data as possible from the Rome lab, and draft a preliminary report for Paul and his superiors. He couldn't help thinking that this result was another of those "minor miracles."

The six of them adjourned to the hotel bar for a few celebratory rounds. McCormack called the lab and ordered the further tests. The mood was upbeat and relaxed; somehow, each of them believed that the lab would report their subject was a man of middle eastern origin, perhaps even with Mediterranean roots. If that were true and to a person they were confident that it was - then it would not be that great a stretch to believe they had found Jesus.

———

The next couple of days were pretty hectic. The lab confirmed their belief that the dna donor was a middle eastern/Mediterranean male. The team members each contributed a section of the preliminary report and John wrote a brief executive summary. He turned it over to Paul, who hand-carried it to the Papal Secretary and delivered it to him in person. Paul's contractors disassembled the temporary lab. Paul escorted Matt and Maria on an extensive insider's tour of the Vatican, where they got to see and enjoy so many works of art and holy relics not usually available to visitors. John tagged along, mostly just to share this special time with his wife. McCormack noticed, more than once, that they were holding hands.

Paul had not forgotten Renee. One evening he took her to dinner, followed by a very personal tour of St. Peter's. They visited the Apostle's suspected tomb, and wondered if, when alive, Peter would have recognized the Suderium man. They could never know, of course, but both of them believed it might be so. Later, they were dwarfed by Bernini's great altar, and she was awed by the interior of the immense dome, drawing the eyes inexorably upward toward...God? There was power in this place, overwhelming wealth and beauty, but was there truth? For that matter, was there truth in science? In the end, she thought, they were just different ways of knowing. For her there had never been a choice; it was always science. She wondered how he had chosen God? She was glad he had because none of this could have happened without him, and she felt very warm and human standing beside him now. She would have very little trouble keeping company with this man. Too bad. She would soon be back in Boston and he would be an ocean and a continent away...

Marty Thomas continued to have his doubts, but he had expressed them to the team and he was satisfied, for the time being, to leave it there. After all, what they had done was done in secret and their conclusions were known only to them, to Paul McCormack, and whoever had access to them at the Vatican. A truly limited audience. And, in the end, it made little difference, in his mind, if the guy of the cloth was Jesus or not. They had gotten to the end point, made their report, and that was the end of it. Real science is fruitful, he thought. What was the fruit of their work in Italy and Spain? They had used science, but had they actually produced anything useful? Well, he thought, maybe all this means something to the Pope...

The next day, their last in Rome, Dr. Thomas had a chance to find out first hand. They had a short private audience with John Paul III himself. It was pretty awesome, even for those among them who were non-believers. His Holiness met them in an ante-room of the Basilica. They had been ushered in before his arrival and when, after a few minutes, he entered, his commanding presence left no doubt that he was the man in charge. But he also radiated warmth and kindness and not a little personal charm. Father McCormack knelt and kissed his ring. The Pontiff blessed them, thanked them for their work, shook their hands...and departed through the door he had just entered. Not a word of why he had supported their work, not a word of what, if anything, he planned to do with it, and certainly no opportunity whatsoever to ask a question. Paul led them out of the room and back into the Cathedral without comment. And that was it. The next day, they were back in Boston, an anticlimactic ending to a couple of weeks that none of them was likely to experience ever again...

CHAPTER 11

Cloning a Human Being was almost inconceivable. Almost. As a genetic researcher, John had been troubled by that issue for many years. In concept, at least, it could be done. The technology was available and it had been applied, with varied degrees of success, to higher animals - notably sheep. The question wasn't so much how to do it as to whether it **should** be done at all. The literature was full of scientific, philosophic and religious commentary and they tended to converge on a single common response: Don't do it. John knew the arguments well; he had, himself, from time to time, been an active participant in the debate, always urging caution and restraint, but never quite willing to dismiss it out of hand. Even so, it was hard for him to ignore the points made by an almost universal opposition. Bad enough, said some, that man was playing God with genetic engineering and cloning animals, but how could he dare do this with his own species? We might now have the ability, but did we have the wisdom to micromanage who we are? What might we create with this technology? Specialized human subspecies, for better or worse? An improved homo sapiens that could supplant us and inherit the Earth with who knows what consequences? And who would get to make these decisions - what to create and to what ends? That was really at the heart of the debate - who would make the decisions once (or if) the proverbial cat was let out of the bag? Certainly there were already tremendous positive dividends arising out of genetic research. But like all science, there were potential dangerous, even disastrous, consequences, too. Splitting the atom was comparable to unlocking the secrets of the gene, it was argued, and mankind has spent almost a century trying to limit and control nuclear weapons, trying to stuff Pandora back into her box. That particular argument didn't impress John very much, because if you wiped out our understanding of the atom in order to avoid stockpiles of nuclear bombs, you would also wipe away a long list of medical, technological and intellectual accomplishments founded upon nuclear physics. Moreover, one might argue that the atom bomb ended one war, and the fundamental unacceptability of any nuclear warfare has served to prevent it from happening again (at least so far!). In the end, John knew, both good and bad things result from applied scientific research. In all likelihood, human cloning, if it was ever done, would follow that well-established principle.

It was no surprise, then, that John had toyed with the idea of producing a human clone as part of what he now thought of as The Jesus Project. It was in the back of his mind when he had submitted his original request to the Vatican. It stayed there, unspoken, while the research was going on. When he got back home and replicated the Roman lab findings, confirming that he had the complete genetic makeup of a man who died almost 2000 years ago, the submerged idea resurfaced. He'd actually tossed up a trial balloon with Renee and Marty, the other "hard" scientists on the team. They'd had a semi-serious conversation about reproducing the man who could be Jesus. Ignoring, for the moment, the fact that it would be unethical and illegal, and brushing aside the religious and philosophical considerations, Renee chose to address the notion from a purely practical perspective. Cloning any mammal was risky, she noted. You had perhaps a 1 in 100 chance of producing a live birth. Then the odds were heavily weighted against this 1 in 100 animal's survival to adulthood. The record was clear. Cloned animals typically had significant problems with both the form and function of internal organs and rarely lived to a reproductive age. There was very little reliable information about what might result if they **did** reproduce, but what was available was not encouraging. The dysfunctions had a tendency to be passed along to the next generation. So, from Renee's perspective, cloning a human being, any human being, was a bad idea.

Dr. Thomas shared her skepticism, and added a few points of his own. First of all, they had no idea exactly who's dna they had captured in Valencia. Could be a congenital mass murderer for all they knew. There was no way of knowing if the donor would want to be cloned. If, by chance, it **was** Jesus, what would his clone be like? "I'm a confirmed agnostic, John," said Marty, "but what if we're actually fooling around with the divine? God only knows - literally - what could happen. Let that thought go for a minute. Let me ask you, John: What, exactly, would you expect to achieve by cloning this man? Nature versus nurture? Without some reliable baseline, without actually **knowing** who our man was and how he lived, there's no way you can answer that question. So, from a purely scientific point of view, why do you want to do this? What is there to be gained?"

John got the message. Not only was he outnumbered, he was out-argued. There really was no justifiable scientific reason to continue the conversation. He wasn't that attached to the notion, anyway. They really didn't know anything substantive about the dna donor. They couldn't possibly know what to expect from a successful cloning. And the likelihood of producing a fully functional human being seemed remote. In any case, Dr. Baptista was not that adventurous; he was unwilling to risk his hard earned reputation or his impeccable professional credentials on rogue research applications. In fact, John had no trouble at all tucking the idea away in a back corner of his brain and he concurrently stored away those chains of dna that he had so carefully cultivated. The idea and the materials would remain locked away for some time to come.

There was a time, some years back, when John and Maria Baptista, newly wed, thought seriously about children. Both of them had been raised in fairly large Catholic families, John in New Bedford and Maria in nearby Fall River, Massachusetts. John's family was third generation Italian. His paternal grandparents had come to America looking for a better life and they had found it. They worked hard, he as a laborer and she as jewelry piece worker, and with their savings they were able to set up their only son, Antony - John's dad - in the construction trade. He started small, but as the business prospered, he married his local sweetheart and they produced a half dozen little Baptistas. John's older brother eventually took over the business and continued to grow it successfully, which suited John perfectly. John had absolutely no interest in construction. His forte was his mind. He excelled as a student and by the time he reached his Junior year in high school it was clear that he had a real future in science. His dad and his brother were genuinely pleased for him and proud of his academic accomplishments. They took it upon themselves, unasked, to provide all the resources necessary for John to enjoy - and take advantage of - a top quality undergraduate and graduate education.

John chose the pre-med program at Brown, but ultimately decided not to become a practicing physician. He had discovered that medical research provided him with greater challenges and, if not the prospect of greater financial rewards, the opportunity to pursue his own clinical interests. He did his doctoral work at Johns Hopkins and a post graduate fellowship in genetics at Harvard. From there he was hired to direct the genetics research laboratory

- and, of course, enabled to do his own original research - at the University where he continued to the present.

John first met Maria at Brown. Her background was Cape Verdian and her family was well-established around Southeastern Massachusetts, where their forbearers had first arrived in this country over 100 years ago. From early days, she was the bright star of her family, smart, personable, social, athletic and down-right cute. Her conservatively Catholic family worshiped at the magnificent St. Anne's Cathedral, and thus from her earliest days she was exposed to a glorious world of artistry and iconography, from the heavenly stained glass, to the Renaissance-style paintings and sculpture, to the masterfully-illustrated texts. As a young child she was captivated. As she grew, her love of art and art history grew along with her, and, ultimately, it became clear that this would be her life's work. She began her post-secondary education at the Rhode Island School of Design and completed her graduate education at Brown. It was there, in her first graduate semester, and John's next-to-last of undergraduate school, that they met. They'd liked each other from the start, enjoyed each other's company, and by the end of the academic year they had become fast friends. They kept in touch and whenever John drove up from Maryland to spend time at home, they got together. Toward the end of his doctoral work, he found himself coming to visit her whenever he could get away, and she, now a recent graduate, visited him as well. By the time he found himself in Boston doing post-doctoral work, she was an assistant curator at the Museum and it was not long before their friendship, which had evolved along the way into a serious love, resulted in marriage.

Within the first few months of their marriage, they considered having children. Their promising professional careers were off to a good start; they could count on an excellent income; and they planned to put down roots and stay in Boston. They were not especially worried about the impact a child would have on their careers or their lives. They could comfortably afford a top-flight nanny and parent around their jobs to the best of their ability. Having come from big families, with lots of little kids around, they began to eagerly look forward to having at least one of their own. But it was not to be. Try as they might - and they did try mightily - Maria never became pregnant. They debated fertility treatments and actually underwent some preliminary testing, but in the end they decided to let nature take its course. If there was to be a little Baptista, it would not be by in vitro. Over time their careers and many other interests displaced their dreams of parenthood. Until now.

Maria's 40th Birthday. The friends were celebrating with dinner at the Top of the Hub. John, who would reach this benchmark himself in a few months, raised his glass and proposed a toast: "May the next 40 be every bit as good as the first. Even Better. I love you, Maria."

Renee chimed in. "We all do," she said, and Martin and Matt offered "Here, here" and "Cheers."

Except for Maria and her husband, spouses were notably absent. In fact, there were none. Careers and circumstances had kept the others unattached. Perhaps that was why, over the years, these five very different people had continued not only to socialize together, but to be truly good friends. They could confidently share their most private thoughts without having to worry about the consequences. Attentive listening, support when needed, and confidentiality were the unwritten rules, and everyone knew them intuitively and honored them. In the immortal words of some long-dead comedian, they were "a really good group."

The after-dinner conversation was relaxed and rather mundane. Who had seen what shows, and were they worth the price of admission? A couple of good books got fast reviews. John's 40th came up, and they talked about how each of them was approaching mid-life in full stride. The talk moved, almost unavoidably, into reflections on hopes and regrets. Renee shared that she felt she was perfectly adapted to urban life as a single professional woman, but she still thought that at some point she might have a husband if the right man came along. Not so much a lover as a companion into her later years. "Oh, by the way, did you know that Paul McCormack is coming back to Boston? Whatever he was doing in Rome is finished and he's been reassigned to the Archdiocese here. We keep in touch, and he told me he'll be landing at Logan in a couple of weeks." She thought fondly of him; he could have been the one - but he chose God. Damned priest!

Marty and Matt allowed that they were perfectly happy with their bachelor lifestyles. They loved their work, their freedom to do as they pleased without the constraints of family, and they certainly didn't miss the prancing of little feet - and all the responsibilities that came with it. There was plenty of loving to be had without any commitment at all and both of them found those short term relationships to be quite sufficient. No, life was good as they were living it; let somebody else commit to permanence and procreation...

Which is exactly what John and Maria had again begun to think about - having a child. They weren't getting any younger and they both felt they wanted to give it one more try. They wanted this - possibly even needed it - to answer to their most basic sense of the meaning of life; to bring a child into the world, to love it and nurture it - to fulfill one's most essential role in the circle of life. Maria's Birthday proved to be the immediate stimulus for much of what followed.

CHAPTER 12

John's Birthday, some month later, was celebrated at home. A quiet dinner with friends, prepared and served by Maria, followed by Black Forest Cake and coffee. Renee had stopped at the bakery to pick it up on the way over. Marty and Matt had each provided a bottle of wine. They noticed, during the meal, that Maria drank water. They had both brought red - cabernet and merlot - perhaps she would simply have preferred something lighter. Whatever...it was another of many good times among friends, and the conversation was appropriately amiable and relaxed. Renee mentioned that Paul McCormack had, in fact, arrived in town. She had had lunch with him a couple of times and he was settling in at the Archdiocese. He was to have an administrative rather than a ministerial role, and he seemed quite happy with that assignment. She had mentioned John's Birthday dinner, but Paul declined her invitation. She thought he might have considered himself too much of an outsider to show up, more or less unexpected, at a fairly intimate gathering of friends. He had, however, simply said he had other things to attend to. He did send along his best wishes, and Renee was more than happy to be his messenger.

John looked lovingly at Maria. He listened absently as Renee delivered Paul's greetings. He was thinking back on the last several months. It had been a difficult time, and Renee had been helpful more than he and Maria might ever have reasonably expected. In fact, she had been essential, and she had kept their confidence in spite of all the nagging issues that had arisen. Hell, some of them were still out there. Nonetheless, Renee continued to support and encourage. God, she was a good friend...

On the night of Maria's Birthday, after all their friends had left, John and Maria found themselves sitting beside one another in the parlor. It was quiet, the lights were dimmed, and they were enjoying the afterglow of a very pleasant evening. After a few minutes lost in their own thoughts, John spoke. "Do you really think we should give it another try? I know it's been on your mind a great deal lately." She nodded, encouraging him to continue. "Well, maybe something has changed in the medical technology since we tried before. Maybe as we've aged there's been some physical change in our bodies. It's certainly not too late to give it another try." Maria offered only silence in response; clearly she was thinking, too.

That night, John had a dream, one that he woke from sweat through. All he could remember was a voice, disembodied he thought, slowly repeating the words "It is time..." It was most troubling, but he had a pretty good idea what his dream was telling him. In the morning, over breakfast, he picked up the previous evening's one-sided conversation. "It's not too late, you know, Maria. There's plenty of time for you to be a mother and for us to raise a child before we're too old to be effective parents. But if we're going to do it, we need to get going again." He reached across the table and put his hand on hers. "I don't want to put pressure on you. I don't even want you to think I am, because I'm not. I want you to be happy for the rest of your life, and I just think you might regret not trying again." You're right, John, she thought; but she wasn't quite ready to speak the words. There had been so much frustration and disappointment in the past. Would it really be worth it to try again? John kissed her and departed for the University. She sat for a few more minutes, nursing her coffee, then headed off to the Museum. What **do** I really want? Her head throbbed. I just don't know.

Maria had trouble focusing on her work that day. For someone who was ordinarily in complete control, that in itself was most bothersome. Several times she found herself in one or another of the galleries staring absently at a portrait of some long-ago mother and her child. She felt as if the paintings were trying to help her make a decision, but she just wasn't quite sure what they were telling her. She battled her way through the work day. By the time she got home that evening she was exhausted and stressed. She told John to order out for dinner, took a quick shower, dried her hair and went to bed. In the morning she awoke early and rose feeling refreshed and decisive. In the night she had heard John's voice. She didn't know if it was a dream or if he was lying beside her whispering softly. "It is time," he said, and she knew he was right. When John joined her for coffee she told him she was ready to try again. He held both her hands and looked deeply into her eyes to see if she really meant it. He was satisfied. "Let's do it," he said.

Over the next weeks they revisited the state of the art fertility clinic that had assessed them years before. They subjected themselves to all the necessary examinations and lab work. They exposed their most intimate selves to evaluation. Sadly, they were told, nothing had changed in their biology. His body was incapable of producing viable sperm and her eggs were infertile. They advised strongly against any kind of in vitro or implantation and would refuse to involve themselves in such a procedure should the Baptistas choose to ignore that recommendation. The technical reasons were relevant only in relation to possible remedies, and apparently there were none. Although the tools available to reproductive specialists had become more sophisticated and more reliable over the years, none of them offered any hope to the Baptistas. They sought a second opinion with the same disappointing and discouraging results. Maria, in particular, felt defeated and depressed. Her powerful emotional reaction to the findings troubled John more than the findings themselves - though he, too, had certainly hoped for a better outcome. Maybe there was still a glimmer of hope. John was just not ready to give up, to leave Maria feeling so defeated. He knew what he had to do. He would talk to Renee. Maybe she could help. Maybe she **would** help.

In addition to her academic and research work as a biochemist, Renee used her Medical degree to pusue her personal interest in women's reproductive rights. It was a cause to which she had become firmly committed during her college days in response to seeing too many unwanted pregnancies among her classmates. There had to be a better way to prevent conception; avoid, if possible, the potential physical and emotional damage to women that might come with abortion of the the pregnancy; and minimize the destruction of a living fetus. She discovered Planned Parenthood, and had done volunteer work there ever since. She was well-respected among those who knew of her long-term commitment for the services she performed without financial compensation. She believed that the help she provided for counteless women over the years was compensation enough.

Her work at Planned Parenthood had unavoidably introduced her to the reproductive problems of some of her patients and their need for low-cost and readily available assistance in dealing with them. It was not long before she had associated herself with a commmunity fertility program that did its best to address some of those problems. John and Maria knew, of course, about all of Renee's extracurricular activities. The topic ocassionally arose in their conversations, but never more than casually. And never, ever in the context of John and Maria's reproductive struggles. They had the best professionals money could buy working to solve their problems, and their problems were of the most intimate and personal nature. Not the stuff of ordinary conversation among even close friends. Renee, for her part, was aware of how much Maria had wanted to be a mother and that she and John had run out of options long ago. She was unaware of their current efforts until John approached her...

John pulled Renee aside the next morning at the lab. She was a little surprised that he had come to her for help, but she was immediately receptive. She had more than an inkling of what her friends had been doing for the last few weeks, and she'd guessed from Maria's unusual moodiness on the couple of occasions they'd gotten together that it hadn't been going well. She told John that she'd be more than happy to help in any way she could. As John's abbreviated recounting of their clinical history unfolded, she'd asked a couple of direct questions about procedures and findings, but was otherwise silent. She knew the clinics and the medical people the Baptistas had seen, and she knew they were the best, not just in Boston but just about anywhere. She also knew that their results were indisputable. Ordinarily she might have suspected the accuracy of a patient's description of his treatment, but John was a clinical professional himself, so she was sure that he'd provided her with accurate information and her questions had simply served to clarify a couple of points in his account. No, from the Baptistas' perspective, the reproductive possibilities were..., well, bleak to non-existent. She could only confirm for John what he and Maria already knew.

John shocked her with his response. "How about cloning?" After a moment she said, "You're kidding, John. If you're not kidding me, you're kidding yourself. You know as well as I do how risky - how damned near impossible - it would be to clone a human being in the best clinical conditions." Her voice was rising as she spoke in a tone of disbelief. She took a breath, exhaled, and said, slowly and softly, "John, I know how hard this must be for you and Maria, but this is beyond the pale...you really need to stop and think about it. I'm your friend, John, and I would help you any way I can. Right now, the best way I can help you is to tell you to stop and think." She patted him on the shoulder gently, turned away and walked slowly back to her office.

It didn't end there, of course. Later that day, John knocked on Renee's door and entered to find her reading a current Journal article on the state of SCNT research. As a geneticist, SCNT was quite familiar to John - it stood for Somatic Cell Nuclear Transfer, and it was one of several viable means to clone living tissues. Evidently, their brief conversation that morning had gotten her thinking. John, for his part, had never stopped thinking about it all day. In fact, he had thought the thing through and now he was ready to share his thoughts with Renee. Given what she was reading, perhaps she was ready to hear him out...

CHAPTER 13

" Alright, said Renee, " Let's talk, **hypothetically**, about how you could clone a human being. Let's begin with a serious review of the literature. Let's take a look at our own genetic and biochemical research for relevant applications. Let's consider the science, the technology and the medical knowledge and competence required to do it. First, though, let's just focus on whether it is a realistic **possibility**. Let's set aside any concerns for how to do it, whether it should be done, who might be a willing and biologically-fit host, or whose genetic material should be used. Let's not worry about whether it's morally right or technically legal. Let's just take your question head on: 'How about cloning?'" She was absolutely confident that they'd never have to address all these non-clinical questions. John would find - they would find - that cloning a human being with any degree of confidence in the result was just not possible.

As it turned out, Renee, who started out with such certainty in her views, was wrong. She had only proposed this route to help John get through a difficult time, to help John get a grip on himself. Surely, he would become convinced that it couldn't be done; the scientist in him would overrule the emotional human being. She was wrong on both counts. Worse, at least from her own perspective, she began to waver in her certainty...

They knew that Dolly the sheep had been cloned successfully in 1996 using SCNT, and since that time several other mammals had been cloned using the same method. Somatic Cell Nuclear Transfer is simple in concept. Nuclear dna is taken from a donor and planted into a host egg cell from which all the genetic material has been removed. The genetic material from the donor is fused to the egg cell by use of an electric current. Once the two cells have fused, the resulting cell is either implanted in a host animal or grown artificially in the lab. This simple process required patience, competence, and the right equipment to accomplish. John had actually replicated it several times in his genetics lab, first for the pure science of it, then as a demonstration and introduction to advanced genetic research for his graduate students.

Human cloning had a clinical history going back over 20 years. In 1998, a commercial research laboratory had created a human embryo using SCNT. They had taken a man's cell and inserted it into a cow's egg. The hybrid cell was cultured in the lab and developed into an embryo. The embryo was destroyed after a couple of weeks of observed development. Ten years later, another bio-tech company succeeded in creating the first fully-human cloned pre-embryos. They used a male skin cell and a human egg with the nucleus removed. They cultured blastocysts, the first stage of the development of a mammal embryo, for several days and then destroyed them in the process of conducting stem cell research. SCNT has since been used to create human stem cells from adult, rather than fetal, donors and to allow biologists to observe the early development of humans in a unique and previously unavailable way. Although the research focus has been on stem cells and embryonic development, the procedures used, now standard and reliable, actually lend themselves to the possibility of cloning a complete human being. A number of researchers have concluded that it can be done with a fair likelihood of success, and a very few have suggested they are in the process of or might actually do it.

Rather than discouraging John, as Renee had hoped, their findings caused him to ask the next and obvious question: Did they have the skills and resources necessary to produce a human clone? Even Renee had to admit that, between the two of them, they certainly did. They had the requisite competencies, access to the necessary labs and equipment and direct control over the research that took place in those labs. John was, of course, a skilled geneticist and Renee had the medical credentials and fertility center connections to enable an implantation and manage a resulting pregnancy. Yes, she was forced to agree, they could do it. But, my God, should they? What was she thinking? Yet she allowed herself to continue to participate in John's exploration of the almost unthinkable...

She **did** try, once again, to put a stop to John's growing enthusiasm for his crazy idea. She enumerated an entire list of practical problems that they would face, along with the potential for disaster along the way. There would be issues for sure; just a few of them might include: For the SCNT process to work, the donor had to be male. Who would it be? How would you select him? A relative? From a sperm bank? At random? Who would decide? What would the selection criteria be? (John had a way to obviate these questions, but he wasn't ready to share it with Renee just yet).

What about the host? Not only would she suffer the ordinary physical and emotional effects of pregnancy, she would be subject to the constant knowledge and anxiety that something could go wrong. A spontaneous abortion at any point was well within bounds, if not likely. The fetus could have other flaws, not necessarily fatal but nevertheless making it necessary to terminate the pregnancy. Or the host could come to full term and deliver a child with any number of physical or developmental problems. How would the mother deal with that outcome? Hell, how would her husband deal with it, especially if he were directly responsible for the process?

There were any number of practical questions. Renee cited just a few. Could it be done in secret? Should it be done in secret? Probably, because if what they were doing became known it would have huge consequences. It could end up in the news and on the web and become the center of controversy. They might be the subject of criminal investigation, possibly charged with a felony. Aside from the financial cost of attorneys and potential incarceration, there would be the impact on jobs and careers - none of it positive, for sure.

John's response to this almost overwhelming list of objections was: "All well taken, Renee. But there is a plus side to consider. Imagine what could be learned from carrying a cloned human fetus to term? There are so many scientific questions that could be raised and answered,both in regard to the fetus and the host - I won't even try to enumerate them. And if the birth is a success, imagine tracking that child's intellectual, physical and emotional development. It's really uncharted territory, and it would be ours to explore."

"But let's go back to the beginning for a minute, Renee. What this is really all about is Maria and I having a child. It's about my love for my wife and her desire to be a mother before it's too late. Somebody will clone a human being one of these days and perhaps open the door to an amazing new reproductive option for everyone. It's almost sure to happen, but it probably won't happen soon enough to help Maria and me. We have the tools, you and I; we have the skills. Why not just do it ourselves, here and now?"

Renee found herself actually beginning to entertain the idea. But she had one more question. It was the most critical question she could think of: "John, does Maria know about this?"

CHAPTER 14

M aria's immediate reaction to John's plan was incredulity; her immediate response was total resistance. "My God, John, are you **serious**? Of course I want a child - **our** child. But not like this. No. I'm just not that desperate! I won't even consider it for a minute." End of discussion.

But it was not the end. John **did** think she was that desperate, or at least he had convinced himself that she was. He realized that he had, himself, become desperate - desperate to be a father, desperate to provide Maria with a baby of her own, increasingly driven to put his plan into operation. And there was always, at the back of his mind, the nagging desire to know who he was...who he **is**. He couldn't let it go now. He had to convince her. It helped that he genuinely believed that it was the right thing to do. But she had to want it, too, or it couldn't happen. There was no way that he would ever consider forcing this on her, but he wanted her to make a decision, not simply a reaction. He had to convince her.

It took the better part of a week, but one by one he successfully challenged her rational objections. She had to admit that although there were obvious risks associated with a cloned pregnancy, **any** in vitro-induced pregnancy was inherently more risky than the natural biological process. He guaranteed that both she and the fetus she carried would be constantly monitored and evaluated, and that she and her baby - their baby - would have 24-hour medical support. If there was a significant problem of any kind, the pregnancy could be terminated quickly and quietly. He would personally prepare the implant and Renee would perform the actual procedure. It would be done in a proper fertility clinic's facilities, and Renee would oversee the pregnancy with the assistance of the clinic's medical and laboratory staff. No one would ever know that the fetus she carried was cloned. They wouldn't have to. She could be identified and treated as a regular in vitro patient. Her total negativity became first less strident, then lessened by degrees. Her rational self was becoming lukewarm to the possibility.

Emotionally, though, she felt like a train wreck. How could John put her in this position? How could he have shared all this with Renee without telling her? Was she willing to carry a cloned fetus in the first place - a fetus made of somebody else's genes, a fetus that at best would grow to be like an adopted child? Did she love John enough to do it for him; could she, should she, do it for herself? How would she, brought up a good Catholic girl, albeit one who was now a pro-choice non-practitioner of the Faith, deal with the reality of an abortion? Who would provide the male chromosomes? How would they decide? What would she tell the child if all went well? Would she ever find herself saddled with guilt? Would she regret it forever if she let this chance to be a mother pass her by? How would John handle the stress himself? What might this do to their marriage, to their personal and professional lives? She felt overwhelmed. Reluctantly, she turned to her best friend, Renee Josephson, for help.

She was reluctant because it was evident that Renee had discussed the subject at length with John without either of them letting her in on the secret. She didn't really know where Renee stood - pro or con. That, however, mattered less than her somewhat shaken confidence in her friend. But Maria now needed someone to help her think and feel this thing through, even if, in the end, it went nowhere. All these thoughts and feelings had been aroused and turned loose in her mind and she needed help. Under the circumstances, she thought Renee was her only option. She arranged to meet her friend for drinks that evening. She made no secret of her date, but she asked John to stay home and let her work this thing out on her own...

Renee arrived first and ordered scotch and soda. She was half expecting Maria to be angry and confrontational, and she thought a little alcoholic fortification was in order. When Maria arrived, however, she quickly made it clear that she was more hurt than angry and she asked for an explanation. Renee described how quickly a hypothetical discussion had taken off and how she had tried to dissuade John. She had to admit, though, that she was intrigued by the possibility, until she realized that Maria was not party to John's thoughts. It was then that Renee had insisted that Maria had to be informed and included in the discussion. John understood that if Maria was opposed, he could write off Renee's participation and the whole thing would go bust. That, in a nutshell, was what brought the two women together tonight.

Maria was placated and satisfied. Renee **had** acted as her friend, and, with the air now cleared, Maria was ready to let all the intimate turmoil she felt spill out. As soon as Maria started to talk, Renee knew it was going to be a long, emotional and difficult evening....

They stayed, nursing their drinks, until well past midnight. Nothing was resolved, but everything was shared. For her part, Renee made it clear that, although she had many reservations herself, she thought bringing a cloned fetus to term was possible. She would work with John to make it happen as long as that's what Maria decided. She was not particularly anxious to keep that commitment, but, then, she really didn't think she'd have to. Maria was so consumed with her jumbled feelings that Renee figured that she'd be unable to resolve them. Renee listened, empathized, occasionally advised, but when the two women hugged and went their separate ways, nothing had really changed.

But change was coming. Through the night, Maria tossed and turned fitfully. Sound sleep would not come. Several times she came full awake and then dozed off again. She dreamed. She could not quite capture it in her conscious mind, but it continued through several waking interruptions. She recognized some faces as she drifted from sleep to wake to sleep again. The Pope was there and for some reason she and Father Paul McCormack were chatting with him. Whatever they were talking about, it was okay. Somebody asked, "Is it time?" Then the whisp was gone. She saw herself in the Museum gallery looking at a Late Medieval icon of mother and child. Was that her own face looking back at her? Later, she and John, picnicking. She looked at him and asked, "Do we have time?" He nodded and they began to...do something, something she couldn't quite remember. And so it went, until she came upon an infant, alone, no place or setting - just alone. The infant looked at her and said in a voice she didn't recognize, "It **is** time." A wall tumbled down upon here, crushing the breath out of her. Out of nowhere, John Paul appeared and blessed her and she felt all of her troubles lift and drift away. She slept soundly after that, and in the morning she knew what she would do.

At breakfast she felt almost giddy. She had to ask herself if perhaps she was just hung over. No, she was just fine. Better than fine. She had made up her mind. John came to the table. She took his hands in hers and said, "Let's do it. I think it's time."

This decision created two immediate problems. One was for Renee. What **would** she do when she learned that Maria wanted to go ahead. Her answer was a simple "OK." She still had plenty of concerns and doubts of her own, but she would stand by her commitment to her friends.

The second problem was less easily resolved. Who would provide the genetic material? John and Maria and members of their families were considered and rejected. Too close personally and genetically. Difficult to maintain secrecy within the family. More difficult to explain and justify what they were doing. Someone close but unrelated? More or less the same issues. A random person? Hard to know anything medical or biological about them. Easy access, but way too risky. They could use a sperm bank donor, but that, too, might expose their purpose. Too much legal red tape. Nonetheless, that remained the only realistic possibility. Until John suggested one more possible donor: A dead person. Someone who had no legal standing, someone without relatives, someone who would never recognize his clone or be troubled by having been cloned, someone who would be unknown to any living person. Perhaps someone like the man from Valencia?

Maria and Renee were taken aback. They had not yet even begun to discuss whether the clone was to be male or female, never mind the Jesus contender! Nonetheless, John pressed the point. They **owned** the genetic material. It was available in the lab right now. Almost no one knew they had it, and those very few who did would never learn about the cloning unless John, Maria or Renee let them in on the secret. By all indications, the man had been genetically sound, a good candidate for reproduction. His middle eastern origin would provide him with a complexion not a great deal different from Maria's. His genetic structure had proven to be not at all out of the ordinary - nothing miraculous hidden in the coding - but what if he had been Jesus? What if they had been chosen to bring him back? Yes, a wild thought, but within the realm of the possible...

Maria was certain now. She told them about her dreams and how she now thought she understood their meaning. As bizarre and mystical as it sounded, she felt that she'd been guided to this moment, that she'd somehow been given permission to go ahead. She'd been absolved of guilt or blame. And she was absolutely confident that it would all turn out perfectly. She was convinced that all of this had been somehow revealed, not so much supernaturally or from God, but because it was there in her all the time. Yes, she was as certain as John, now. It was time...

CHAPTER 15

Once the decision was made, things progressed rapidly. Renee provided an egg and John removed the genetic material. He then fused the "Jesus" mitochondrial dna with the egg. The procedure went flawlessly and in 5 days Renee had cultured a viable blastocyst in her lab. A week later it had developed into a microscopic embryo, ready for implantation and capable of survival. Maria was admitted to Renee's fertility clinic, where the actual implantation procedure was performed. It was simple, fast, painless and successful. Renee immediately began a regimen of daily monitoring, blood, urine, sonogram and by the end of the month she could confirm that Maria was indeed pregnant, with, to the extent it could be determined, a normal, healthy fetus. Renee ran every relevant screening test typically applied during the first trimester. After 90 days, the pregnancy was progressing normally. There was still a long way to go, but Renee told Maria this might be a good time to share her news with friends. She did it a couple of days later at John's 40th Birthday party. It really **did** feel wonderful to let them in on her joyful tidings, and it was a hell of a Birthday gift to share with John. They were indeed a happy couple, expectant in more than the typical way, hopeful that the next six months would be as problem-free as the first three.

There was always the unspoken fear, the anxiety lying just below the surface calm, that something **would** go wrong, but it never did. By the end of the second trimester, the sonogram showed a perfectly

81

formed boy with a regular heart beat and normal motive activity. Analysis of amniotic fluids showed no hint of defects in the fetus. It was beginning to appear quite miraculous. They had beaten the 1 in 100 odds of getting a fetus two thirds of the way through gestation without a hint of trouble. The fetal organs had formed correctly and were functioning properly at this stage of development. John was elated, Renee was pleasantly surprised, and Maria, now obviously carrying, remained totally confident. She **knew** it would be alright. Renee just hoped that nothing would happen in the next 3 months to prove that confidence unfounded. Even though things looked really good from a medical point of view, the odds against the delivery of a perfectly formed and perfectly functioning newborn were still very high. Renee kept up the intensity of her monitoring and testing as much to reassure herself as to identify even the slightest hint of a problem. They were past the abortion window; thankfully, it had never been necessary to make a decision about termination of the pregnancy.

Maria's health was amazing, given her age and the fact that this was her first pregnancy. She never suffered morning sickness, her blood pressure had remained near normal, and her heart was strong. She had gained some weight, of course, and would gain some more; but she was not burdened with an excess of water weight. And she was good-natured about all the monitoring, prodding and testing that Renee insisted on putting her through. She never became short-tempered, never lost her even disposition and steady optimism. The baby was fast approaching the point of survivability should Maria prove unable to carry him to term. In the now increasingly unlikely event that this should happen, Renee felt the fetus had already demonstrated a strong will to survive and that it would soon be developed sufficiently and strong enough to survive a premature birth.

John and Renee kept copious notes and records, never sure, however, what they would actually do with them. They would unquestionably provide the basis for a whole series of scientific papers, since virtaully everything they were observing and documenting was new and uncharted territory . At some point they might actually write some of these articles and they would have absolutely no problem getting them published. But they knew that their truly ground-breaking work would probably never see the light of day... at least not in their lifetimes. They would keep their secret, never risk revealing it because of the ethical, personal and professional issues involved; because of the firestorm it might cause for them, for Maria and the child. They might serve as a unique genealogy for the boy should there ever come a time when he was ready to know and understand it. That revelation would take some careful consideration. Perhaps some future medical issue, when the information would be critical, would be the occasion. But who could predict how he might be affected by knowing his heritage? This was something best left lost, permanently, in his past. On the other hand, should cloning human beings ever become an acceptable practice, their records would prove that they had done it first and, just as importantly, provide their son and his descendants with documentation of a true and fantastic blood line...

Maria had early on taken medical leave from the Museum, when it became evident that carrying this baby, with all the associated testing and monitoring, was a full-time commitment. Now she spent much of her time at home reading, relaxing and reflecting. Classical music kept her company, softly, in the background. Books and portfolios laden with high quality images of medieval and renaissance paintings covered the coffee table. Most of them had a religious theme; many of them portrayed the Madonna and Child. Maria felt an ever-growing sense of kinship with the Holy Mother, for, like Mary's, her pregnancy was a truly immaculate conception. She had feared she would feel estranged from the child growing in her womb, but it was not so. She was **his** mother every bit as much as Jesus was **her** son. She loved her little boy and she could actually sense that he returned that love. She was more sure than ever that she would come to full term and deliver a perfect child. She fantasized that they'd all live happily ever after, unless...She feared there might be another kind of connection to Mary, one that, if real, could cast a shadow on the future of her son.

Her ruminations were interrupted by a buzz at the door. Moving a little more slowly and awkwardly than in the first months of her pregnancy, she made her way over and looked through the peep hole. It was Renee, and she had someone with her: Father Paul McCormack. She opened the door, greeted them warmly, and invited them in.

She had not seen Paul since they left Rome. God, that seemed a lifetime ago, but it was actually only something over a year. Paul hadn't changed a bit. He was still the tall, dark, handsome and articulate fellow who had been their chief enabler in Italy and Spain. She wondered for an instant if the Pope had sent him, but quickly dismissed the thought as pure whimsy. No, Renee had told her that Paul had been reassigned to the Boston Archdiocese and now that he'd settled in they were seeing each other quite frequently. Theirs had become a serious friendship. Good for Renee, she thought; just the kind of man she needs, one who will never threaten her with marriage, but one who will probably be around for a long time...

They engaged in pleasant small talk for awhile. Paul was working as a community affairs liaison for the Archbishop. It was not an easy job, considering the long history of pedophilia and cover-up that had plagued the Archdiocese in the past. His boss had been charged with cleaning up the mess, making amends and re-establishing the integrity and credibility of the Church in Boston. Paul was pleased with this assignment and challenged by it. The restoration of faith. That was his priestly view of the task before him and he welcomed it.

"Speaking of the restoration of faith, I understand from Renee that you've lapsed in yours. Now that you're to be a mom, maybe you should reconsider. What you believe will certainly influence what your child believes, and we can't have a lamb left to the wolves, can we now?" He was not proselytizing and she didn't take offense. Actually, it complemented some of her own recent thoughts. But she kept those to herself. To him she said, "Thanks for your concern, Paul. We'll see where it goes." He got the final word: "I've brought you something, a Saint Anne's- medal to protect you and watch over you and your son." Renee took it from him and hung it, on its silver chain, around Maria's neck. "Thank you, Paul. I **will** wear it. It is a kind and thoughtful gift." The conversation drifted off to other things and before too long it was time for Paul and Renee to go. She saw them out, told Renee that she'd see her later at the clinic, and closed the door. She stood there a moment fingering Paul's gift. Yes, she thought, I **will** wear it...then she returned to easy chair, patted her tummy, and fell quickly into a brief but restful sleep...

The next three months sped by, each day that Maria success-fully carried the baby leading to the next. Each passing day less-ened John's anxiety, gave him increasing confidence that his wife was right. Everything would work out perfectly. And so it appeared. There were no problems with the baby, no problems with the preg-nancy and no problems with Maria. It had turned out, dare he say 'miraculously,' to be an absolutely normal gestation and the end was in sight.

Over the months, John had done some reflecting of his own. He had never told Maria about **his** "prophetic" dream. He hadn't given it much credence at the time, no more, really, than he had given Maria's - and that was none. But now he wasn't so sure. Everything had gone too well, too perfectly. They had anticipated and prepared for all kinds of potential crises and disasters, but none ever materialized. He had now begun to believe that none ever would. John wondered if he, himself, was the principal author of all the events that culminated in this pregnancy, or if there might actually be something else at play. It all appeared so neatly packaged: The unexpected approval to study the shroud, the discovery of the Valencia cloth, the dna, Maria's barrenness and John's inability to do anything about it, their desire for children, his and Renee's professional knowledge and competencies, the easy availability of clinical support, the easy and problem-free pregnancy...and so many other things. Probably all coincidental, he thought, but what were the odds? It really didn't matter. He and Maria were going to have a son...

CHAPTER 16

Renee and Paul visited Maria together a half dozen times over the next couple of months. All of the visits were unscheduled, spontaneous, and intended to provide Maria with social contact and support as she found herself more and more confined, encumbered, as it were, by her "condition." John, who continued working, missed most of these get-togethers; he had graduate students who required his attention, and a lab to run. Renee, on the other hand, had been able to delegate at her lab and she didn't have the burden of advanced students. This had freed her up to monitor the pregnancy and still have time to drop in socially once in awhile.

Renee had never been especially comfortable with what they were doing, but her level of discomfort was never enough to cause her to back out on her commitment to her friends. And she had to admit to herself that her unease had been significantly lessened by the baby's normal development and Maria's success in carrying him. Still, there was much that gave her pause. Mostly, she was troubled by the sense that they were playing God. Renee was not a religious person - at least not in any traditional sense - so her problem was not fear of God. On the contrary, it was fear of man. What would people **do** with this amazing technology once it became available? In spite of ethical and legal concerns, she was pretty sure it **would** become available because it was **human** nature to discover new tools and put them to use. Nothing divine here, but certainly plenty of opportunity for plain old fashioned good and evil! It was well, she thought, that they'd agreed from the start to keep this thing secret. Keep the lid on it, she thought. Maybe we'd get wiser but, unfortunately, things like money, power and ego so often took discoveries like this out of wiser hands and did...God knows what with them. Oh, well, she had long since reconciled herself to seeing Maria through this and that is exactly what she would do.

Paul, for his part, had a sense that something a little out of the ordinary was involved in Maria's blessed event and Renee's continuing active part in it. He was, however, perfectly willing to accept Renee's explanation that as a first pregnancy, given Maria's age and the use of in vitro, all these special precautions were absolutely necessary. She was doing the work herself because she had the facilities and she was Maria's best friend. Still, he had noted all the various religious art work that Maria kept open and about and he wondered if he was missing something. Was this, perhaps, a sign that Maria was discovering spiritual renewal as a consequence of bringing new life into the world? Or was she just falling back on old beliefs to provide her with a bit of emotional comfort? Maybe he was making too much of it. Maybe it was just work that she'd brought home from the museum. Maybe she had lost her faith and needed a way back; maybe he could be that bridge. He chose not to pursue it with her and set it aside for now.

The whole crew was there for dinner. Martin had come over from the University, Matt from the Museum and Renee had brought Paul along. John had ordered Chinese, and the table was spread with a diversity of containers. It smelled good, tasted better, and everybody dug in. It was a happy occasion and they were all in a celebratory mood. Just a month left 'til the big day, and Maria already looked full-term. More importantly, she looked and was in fabulous health.

John and Maria passed around sonograms of the baby. It appeared that he was smiling and waving at them. She let them all put a hand to her tummy so they could feel the little guy kicking. Renee took out a stethoscope and let everyone take turns hearing the fetal heartbeat. It was strong and steady. It wouldn't be long now...

"Have you decided on a name?" asked Marty. "He looks like a John Jr. to me," interjected Matt. "Yes, we think he does, too," said John. "Maria and I agree and John it will be. But we haven't landed on a middle name yet and I think it's pretty important that we give him a good one."

"Yes," agreed Marie. "We don't want to have a John-John running around the house, and Junior really lacks something, doesn't it?"

"Do you have any in mind," asked Paul?

"You wouldn't be leaning toward John Paul, would you?" Renee joked.

"No, nothing like that. But something with more than one syllable, for sure," said John.

"Yes, something that sounds nice with John and Baptista, something that lends itself to a reasonable nickname."

"How about 'Kennedy'" someone suggested. "That's perfect for a Boston brat!"

"Joseph? John Joseph? He could be 'JJ'!"

They tossed names back and forth for a few minutes, and John and Maria rejected one after another. They were running out of steam when Paul offered his suggestion. He thought of all the Christian art that so occupied Maria. "How about 'Christian?'" he asked. John thought about the potential irony of such a name, an irony only three of them could entertain. He said nothing. Maria said, "Yes, that's a maybe. Chris. Yes, I rather like it. Let's consider it, John." He nodded, and the conversation moved on to other things.

A week or so later, Paul and Renee were visiting Maria once again. Three weeks to go and Maria was really feeling it now. She was still carrying the baby high, and he was near full-term, so she felt some pressure on her breathing and a tremendous weight pulling her off balance to the front. Her back hurt. For the first time, she was ready for this to be over. Nevertheless, she was happy, as happy as she had ever been. Soon, after all this time and all those past failures, she would be a mother! Yes, she was ready...

And, she told them, she was ready with a name: "John Christian Baptista." John wasn't as enthusiastic for "Christian" as she was, but he was willing to go along with her choice. He could live with "Chris," but in his mind he already heard himself calling, "J.C., where are you?" And in just a couple of weeks, he'd have a son to respond...

CHAPTER 17

M aria was sitting half upright in the Birthing Room bed at Brigham and Women's. Her eyes were closed and she was breathing through a particularly intense contraction. She could hear music, oddly something approximating the hallaluja chorus. As the contraction eased, she opened her eyes. A woman, not her husband John, was holding her hand. Somehow, this didn't startle or upset Maria; on the contrary, it was as if it was only to be expected. She felt comforted. The woman was wearing biblical robes and, if there was any doubt in Maria's mind who that woman was, a halo of light surrounded her head. Her face glowed with kindness and compassion. She was flanked by heavenly beings, white-robed and angelic. Maria smiled. Then, she felt another contraction coming on, closed her eyes and felt Mary's hand tighten on hers. When she opened her eyes, she was alone, seated on the big easy chair in her living room. Just a dream...one of many she'd had over the last week...just another dream...

Later that day, Paul and Renee had come by to take her for a final OB check-up. Renee made a cup of tea for Maria and coffee for herself and Father McCormack. Maria was **huge** now; she looked like she might pop at any minute, so they packed a small "hospital bag," just in case. Maria was anxious to tell them about her dreams, but she managed to keep them to herself. She'd tell Renee when they were alone. She would understand. And Paul really didn't need to know. It might cause him to ask some awkward questions...So, they chatted about nothing very much, finished their coffee and tea, and were on their way.

There was, as always, a wait to see the Doctor. Maria flopped into a chair and Renee handed her a small pile of magazines to look through. Renee picked up one of those medical journals that inexplicably pepper doctors' waiting rooms - perfectly unsuitable material for the average patient, but perfect for Renee - and she started to read. Paul ignored the pile of magazines and turned his attention to the TV screen, mounted high on the wall, and the CNN news. No sound, just captions, so he had to watch attentively. Never seemed to be much **good** news, he mused. A running litany of man's inhumanity, stupidity and ignorance, with barely a mention of the myriad of good that is done by most of the people, most of the time. Inconsequential to the news, perhaps, but real...much more real and relevant to the daily life of mankind...

Maria sorted through her pile of magazines. The usual suspects. A couple of golf titles, a year- old Sports Illustrated, a couple of dated Time, People and a scattering of drug company publications. Absolutely nothing here of interest to her; no distractions to pass the time. She closed her eyes; she was exhausted. The mere effort of carrying herself and Christian to the OB office had taken its toll. She felt herself drifting off...

She answered the insistent ringing of her phone. "Mary here again. Take good care of that boy...I'm watching you..." Maria shook her head. The receptionist had called her name.

"Cervix dilated to 2 centimeters...looking good Maria. Sometime this week, I'd say. Couple of days off yet, probably." The doctor checked her vitals. Blood pressure a little high, but still okay. "Keep a watch on that, Maria. If it runs up much higher, give me a call." Mother's heart and respiration, excellent. Baby's heart, strong and steady. She let Maria listen. It was a wonderful, reassuring sound. They looked at the live-time sonogram. The little guy was almost telling them, "I'm ready to come out." He was just plain beautiful, moving around in there. She thought she saw him smile at her and at that exact moment they captured him in a still frame that she could take home to John. Hi, daddy, she thought. She was filled with happiness...and just a touch of dread. She had never done this before... how would she handle the delivery? Would it hurt? She was sure it would, but she thought she could manage it...John would be by her side...and so, she thought, would her new friend, Mary...

On the way home, Maria shared all the latest medical news. It sounded really good. It would only be a few days now until John Christian Baptista took his first breath of 21st century air. They chatted happily for a few minutes. Then Maria's voice took on a more serious tone. "Guys," she said, "John and I really appreciate what you've done for us. It's more than that. Renee, you're our best friend. And Paul, you've become our friend too. We would like you to be Christian's Godparents. Will you do it? Please..."

CHAPTER 18

"It's time," said John. The words echoed in the back of his mind. It was as if he'd said them - or perhaps just heard them - before. Deja vu? What was it? He shrugged it off.

Maria was packed and ready. "It **is** time," she responded. The words certainly had special meaning to **her**. She was ready. She was confident. She just wanted this to be over with! "Let's get this show on the road..."

John had pulled the car up to the curb in front of the house. He followed her out of the house, closed the door and helped her down the stairs. Getting her into the passenger seat was no easy trick, but they accomplished it without incident. When her water had broken earlier that morning, there had been a few moments of high drama, bordering on the hilarious. First time mothers have all been visited with that instant of recognition, thrill, horror and delight. It was grinch-like she thought, wonderfully awful! But now, all was calm and they were in complete control. No need to rush. There was plenty of time. Renee would meet them at the hospital; Paul would come if he could get away. That really accounted for the whole family: Mom, Dad, Godparents and baby boy. John and Maria held hands as he drove. This had been a long, long journey and they'd arrive at their destination in a very few minutes....

It was late afternoon in Rome. The setting sun illuminated the great dome of the Basilica. Inside, John Paul III was preparing for evening prayers. One of the assisting priests called out, "It is time, your Holiness." A fleeting thought passed through the Pontiff's mind. "Yes," he said, "perhaps it is."

Back in Boston, Maria had been admitted and was sitting comfortably - or at least as comfortably as strong, regular contractions, would allow - in a large easy chair. John was at her side playing the role of coach as best he could, which he knew, honestly, was not very well. But that didn't matter to Maria. He was holding her hand, and he was there with her, and that's what **really** mattered to her right now. Renee was on her way, and Paul would join them later, as soon as he could get free. The contractions were only a few minutes apart now. Between contractions she would relax, but during them she struggled to focus on a single point in the birthing suite, try to ignore the pain, and breathe fast and hard. She was afraid she might pass out. She wondered if her choice to do this without anesthesia was such a good idea. Too late, now. Finally, after what seemed an eternity, their nurse/midwife approached them and said, "It's time..." She helped Maria get up on the bed and checked her cervex. 8 centimeters. Maria thought "Thank God, it won't be long 'til this... another contraction violently interrupted her thought...

Paul was anxious to get away, but he could hardly show any impatience. He was talking with one of the victims, trying to get a first-hand understanding of how it had happened. Trying to be consoling and empathic when he suspected that this young man had

had enough of priests and probably felt that Paul was completely disingenuous. It was not an easy thing - for either of them. This was a fairly typical case. The man, now approaching middle age, had been assaulted many times over the years, starting when he was a choir boy. His parish priest had told him he was special, that God wanted him to do it, and that he could never tell anyone. But he did tell, and no one believed him. Just the opposite. His parents punished him and told him never to bring it up again. No one ever challenged the priest, so it went on for years. When the boys grew up, several of them convinced their parents and their parents went to the Bishop. He dismissed the allegations for years, until the number of complaints was overwhelming. Then he simply reassigned the offending priests to a different parish. This, he hoped, would be the end of the tale, but, in the end, only the beginning. Many of these pedophiles could not control their impulses and inclinations and they continued their activities with boys in their new assignments. The parents - and, by this time, the adult boys - had seen enough. Law suits followed, heads rolled, settlements were made; priests were disrobed, several went to prison, and the Archbishop was reassigned to the Vatican. But settlements and reassignments did little to fix the damage, both to the lives of the boys and the credibility of the Church. Paul was part of an effort to try to make things right, to really listen to the victims, show them that the culture of the Church had changed, that it was worthy of their faith once more. Engaging the victims in constructive dialogue was part of the process; it was not easy and more frequently than not, unrewarding. It is hard to change minds; harder, still, to change hearts. But Paul soldiered on...

As the interview finally came to an end, Paul found himself thinking of rebirth and renewal. That's what his Church needed; "Hell," he thought, "after being involved in all this, I need rebirth and renewal." Rebirth and renewal filled his brain with a plethora of random but related thoughts as he headed for Brigham and Womens'. There, he thought, he would at least find newborn innocence. Yes, new beginnings, but always built on the remains of the old. What was that song? "Every new beginning is some other new beginning's end..." He hailed a cab and was on his way.

Back at the Birthing Room, Maria's contractions were coming every minute. She was fully dilated. It was time. She could feel her body working to deliver him, she could feel her son reaching for the light. A big push...a monster contraction...push, breathe...push hard....and then.. it was over. John cut the cord, the midwife clamped it, there was a slap and a small outcry, and in a brief moment, John Christian Baptista was curled on her chest. He was slightly blue and bright pink all at the same time, and covered in birth fluids, but his face was clean. He was absolutely beautiful, angelic she thought. He had dark hair, and quite a bit of it, but, because it was wet and milky, she couldn't tell if it was brown or black. His eyes were brown, she was sure of **that**. He **touched** her with his tiny hand and she fell instantly and forever in love with him.

The midwife took him and weighed him. 7 pounds 7 ounces. His APGAR was a 10 - good color, good respiration, good movement. She reassured Maria, who was recovering from the delivery and simultaneously trying hard, without much success, to watch the midwife and see her son, that he was all there - perfect. Maria wanted him back. She held him to her breast and, tentatively at first, then with a little more assurance, he began to suckle. The midwife draped a light blanket over him, and he stayed on her chest, touching and grasping with his little fingers, until it appeared that he had dozed off. Being born is hard work, she thought - almost as hard on him as on me...maybe more so. She hummed to him and looked, alternately, from him to John and back again. Smiling all the while.

———————

Paul and Renee were in the room now. Maria had passed the afterbirth and was relaxing, still in bed, sipping a ginger ale. The baby was in an incubator in the neo-natal unit. Maria had hated to part with him, but the midwife convinced her that it was best for both of them, mother and child, to get some rest. After the initial thrill of the birth had passed, John could not keep himself from wondering just who his son might **really** be - besides being his son, of course, because John had long since accepted his impending fatherhood. There was nothing he could see that might indicate that Jesus, himself, had returned to the world. No halo, no angels, no heavenly choir - and, as a scientist, he had expected none. But he had rather hoped there would be some indication... Perhaps the problem-free pregnancy and the perfect little child was evidence enough. How unlikely was it that everything would go as smoothly as it had? Improbable, for sure. Miraculous?

Renee looked at John questioningly. He understood. He shook his head no. He was careful not to let Paul see their brief interaction.

After that, it was all congratulations and great cheer in the Birthing Room. Maria had done well. They all had done well. And John Christian was a perfect baby boy!

———————

In Rome, it was late night, approaching dawn. His Holiness woke and for a moment tried to remember what he'd been dreaming. Something about the rising sun...but he was unable to get a grip on the thought, and he drifted back into a deep sleep.

CHAPTER 19

John and Renee had adjourned to the Hospital cafeteria, ostensibly for coffee, but actually for a brief private conversation. Renee wanted to know if John had noticed anything - anything at all - unusual about his son. He told her he had not. He shared his earlier thoughts with her about the low probability that the whole thing, from cloning to delivery, would go so flawlessly, but, he asked her, "Does that constitute a miracle? I really don't think so. For all we know, if we cloned a dozen different individuals and implanted them in a dozen different hosts, the results would be the same. Or all of them could be a disaster. We really have nothing but animal studies to go on."

Renee said, "There's absolutely nothing out of the ordinary in his biology, but I can reiterate what you just said: We have no idea about the biology of the real Jesus, so there's really no way of knowing if it is him we've cloned." In one sense, it didn't matter at all, because John and Maria had a healthy little boy. In addition, John and Renee had kept extensive scientific records that might prove useful for future researchers, given the right circumstances. But in some sense, for want of another word, a spiritual sense, they wondered if they had participated in a sort of modern day resurrection? They could only conclude that time would tell and they would be on hand, one as a father, and the other as a friend, to see what happened.

Back in the room, Paul and Maria were engaged in a private conversation of their own. Paul proposed to take his role as Godfather literally. That is, he wanted to insure that Christian was brought up in the Catholic faith, and he, Father McCormack, wanted to play a guiding and supportive role. A year ago, Maria would have politely disabused him of any such notion. She was only nominally Catholic, had not been near a church, except for weddings and funerals, in years. She loved the art and the music, even the traditional liturgy. But she could, and did, have total access to the art and music via her professional career, the great museums and books and recordings. As to the liturgy, the beautiful traditional Latin, it was a thing of the past. The secularized version appealed to her not one whit. The truth was all she really needed was humanity; the divine might be a necessary component of great artistry, but it was otherwise not a part of her life.

Or so she thought. Now, however, looking back on a truly incredible and wondrous year, she wasn't so sure. She had actually felt herself touched by - --what? The angels? The Madonna? Certainly by something that at least hinted at the divine. From the beginning, she had been told the odds were stacked against them at every stage, but there had been no problems at all. None. And now she had a perfect little boy. She wasn't ready to tell Paul - she might never be ready - but she wondered if all of it, from the approval to study the Shroud, right on to Paul's current proposal, might not be pre-ordained. Maybe something miraculous **was** going on and maybe she and her son were at the center of that miracle. Yes, maybe Father McCormack was an unknowing part of some larger plan. So she told Paul that she was amenable to his request, but that she would have to take it up with John. There was no way that she would make an important, possibly critical, decision about the future of **their** son without his involvement and concurrence.

About that time, Marty and Matt appeared at the door. Matt brought flowers and candy for Maria. Martin brought a little plush lamb for the baby. The lamb was Christian's first gift, brought by a wise man, she briefly mused. She thanked them and invited them to sit. This brought an immediate end to Paul and Maria's private talk. The four of them began to chat about how Maria was doing and how perfect a child she had produced. Meanwhile, John and Renee's private conversation had also come to an end, and they came back into the room bearing a tray of hot and cold drinks and snacks. The happy group kept up the camaraderie for a little while, then, one by one, they took their leave. Finally it was just Maria and John, alone with the baby.

They sat quietly for a few minutes, exhausted, drained, but not ready for sleep. Christian stirred and whimpered softly. John got up from his chair and stood over the little bundle, looked down at his tiny face peeking out of the blanket that was wrapped around him. The baby stirred again, opened his eyes and turned his head so that he appeared to be looking directly at his father. John thought he saw a faint smile - probably just a belch, he thought, but he returned it with a gentle smile of his own. He picked the baby up ever so carefully and placed him in Maria's arms. She raised him to her chest; he fumbled for a moment, then found a nipple. She could feel his little body relax. In a few minutes he was back to sleep. It wasn't long before John and Maria, he in his chair, she on the bed, had joined him in dreamless slumber.

The next morning, Maria awoke feeling renewed. Christian had awakened several times during the night and she had suckled him, sung to him softly, and he had gone back to sleep. He was sleeping now, breathing quietly and steadily, as she rose from the bed and placed him in the cradle. She held her breath, but he never stirred. John, collapsed on his bedside chair, never stirred, either. She made her way gingerly to the bathroom and looked at herself. Face a bit worn, perhaps, hair a mess, but that huge belly and most of that extra weight were gone. She thought of all those paintings of the Nativity, of how composed and rested Mary looked. **That** was the **real** miracle she thought, smiling at her self-deprecating humor. Actually, she thought, the real miracle was her perfect little boy. He had beaten the odds. He had made it and now he would be a part of their lives forever. "Thank you, Mary" she whispered, and she almost added, "for sharing him with me..."

Maria freshened up, exchanged her hospital johnnie for a nursing gown, and came back into the room. John was just waking, so she sat in the chair next to him. She had for so long flopped, heavily and awkwardly, into chairs that she was amazed at how simple it had become. John reached over to her and they held hands, her left in his right, and he leaned across and kissed her softly. Their baby was a creation of love, a manifestation of love, but love of an unusual kind. He was not in the sexual sense a procreation, especially ironic **if** he carried Christ's genes. Whether he did or not now seemed academic to John. There was no evident sign of inherent divinity in Christian and there probably never would be. No matter who his genetic donor had been, he and Maria had brought him into the world and they would love him and cherish him as their own.

A nurses' aid knocked, then entered the room with two breakfast trays. Coffee, orange juice, scrambled eggs and toast. It looked to John and Maria like a gourmet meal. As they ate, they talked in low voices so as not to disturb their son, who was sleeping peacefully beside them. Maria told John about her conversation with Paul McCormack. His initial reaction - and a reaction it was - was negative. He felt protective of the child and protective of his father-hood. Neither he nor his son needed a meddlesome priest. But that's not how he responded to Maria.

"You and I have lived without the Church for 20 years," he said. "Do we really want to encourage him to be a part of something we have no interest in doing ourselves? I'm sure Paul means well, but proselytizing is not what I had in mind when we asked him to be Christian's Godfather."

"I'm not so sure," said Maria. "We were brought up in the Church and it provided us with structure and values. The divinity stuff, I agree...not so much. But Paul doesn't seem to be a divinity guy. He's more of a humanist, and he **does** have a background in science. Couldn't we just leave it an open question for awhile?"

"Do you want to have the baby Christened?" John asked.

"Yes, if you don't mind too much, I do."

"No, I don't mind," John answered. "Under the circumstances, it actually strikes me as quite appropriate. Maybe you can let Paul officiate, and then we'll see where it goes."

"Fine idea," she replied. "Anyway, he's a priest and he could be reassigned anywhere, anytime, so it might not even be an issue..."

By late that afternoon they were home. Christian was bundled up snugly in the cradle next to their bed and the whole bedroom had been turned into a temporary nursery. That night they all slept, a sound and dreamless sleep. This was the beginning of a whole new life for all three of them...

CHAPTER 20

John Christian Baptista was baptized at the Cathedral of the Holy Cross in Boston's South End. The Cathedral is a huge stone edifice fronting Washington Street. It is the Mother Church of the Archdiocese and His Eminence, the Archbishop, presided. This was a high honor that had been arranged by Father McCormack, who was present to assist in the ceremony. Maria stepped up to the Baptismal Font and held the baby in front of her so that he could receive the blessing of the Church. John Christian was awake and alert. The celebrants noted his full head of dark hair, his big, brown eyes, and his slightly dark complexion. He certainly appeared every bit his mother's child. The Archbishop anointed him, crossed the baby's forehead and spoke the words that welcomed him to the Church and dedicated him to a life of Catholicism. The baby remained silent. Father Paul offered a brief homily, noting how critical a moment this was in John Christian's life and that it was up to his parents, with the help of God and the Church, to guide him forward to his confirmation. There were smiles and handshakes all around, a couple of photos were taken and the Archbishop took his leave.

The little group - Maria, John, Renee and Paul - remained in place for a few minutes, taking in the magnificence of the Cathedral's interior artistry and iconography. Maria held Christian to her breast and felt the caress of his tiny hand. She fixed her gaze on a life-sized statue of Mary and wondered if she had felt the same caress so long ago. Did Mary have any idea what was to become of her son? Probably not, she mused. If the Biblical texts were true, she must have thought that she had given birth to a future king, a true child of God, destined to lead Israel to freedom from Rome. She probably knew nothing about redemption and salvation, just that she was a vehicle for something bigger - much bigger - than herself. Had she foreseen what would happen to her son, would she have allowed it or done all in her power to save him - perhaps even save him from himself? But she didn't know...she couldn't have known. Just look at the pieta at the front of the church, look at her anguish...

Maria felt a sudden sense of dread.

For his part, John was not all that thrilled with the Baptism. A simple ceremony had been elevated way beyond what he thought ws necessary. He was impressed with the Cathedral and the presence of the Archbishop, but he also felt that it was a bit of an imposition to have to come over here, stand before a high Church authority and be subjected to a rather directive, if not downright condescending, homily. He had agreed, somewhat reluctantly, to a Catholic upbringing for his son. A Baptism at the local parish church conducted by the local priest would have suited him better. This was just more than he'd bargained for and it caused him to be concerned about the boy's future. He made a decision...

On the drive home, he asked Maria if she'd thought any more about Christian's education. Before she could respond, he told her, "I want him to have a really good secular education, prep school, college, the best."

She responded with a raised eyebrow and a whispered, "Oh?"

" Maria, I've outgrown my childhood beliefs. You have, too. I don't think we should encumber our son with an unbalanced dose of Catholic faith."

He waited for a response. None came, so he continued.

"I don't doubt for a minute that religious education is a good thing. You learn from an early age about good and evil, right and wrong...that there's something bigger than you, bigger than all of us. You cultivate humility and good conscience. You learn about faith. But you also get exposed to a lot of total nonsense."

Still no response from Maria.

"I've spent more than half a lifetime in science. I use reason to make sense of a world I can measure and test. Science is all about questioning. Science produces results and useful things. In the end, science is about **change**. The Church is all about resistance to change. It's about blind belief. But that's not reallly my point. I want our son to be a rational person, a critical thinker. I want him to be able to make his own considered decisions I want him to have the kind of education that makes that possible."

Maria said, "I understand. I have to agree. Anyway, I don't see any reason why faith and science can't co-exist, do you?"

John was ready to continue pressing his argument, but he saw no reason. She had agreed. An important decision had been made... Christian could go to church, he could be influenced by what he learned there, but he was going to receive a counter-balancing secular education. He would be able, John thought, to think for himself and be free to decide how he would deal with faith and God.

Maria was satisfied, too. She wanted her son to be presented with all the teachings of the Church, in large part because of who she thought he might be; but there needed to be a brake of some kind. She was genuinely concerned about what he might do with those teachings...or what they might do to him. She remembered the dread she'd felt at the Cathedral and goosebumps ran up and down her arms. Yes, John was right; they really would have to provide Christian with a well-balanced education...It was their responsibility...and it was probably part of His plan...

Maria was able to arrange parental leave for six months and she fell into a comfortable routine with the baby. He was normal and healthy in every measurable way. He was alert and responsive; he would follow a moving finger with his eyes, and, when he was in his cradle and Maria approached, he would reach out to her. She nursed him for several months before introducing a bottle. She hated to do it, but she knew she would have to return to work and he had to be prepared for a part-time nanny. Finding the **right** nanny turned out to be a daunting task. They contacted agencies, read resumes and interviewed a couple of applicants, but they found no one with whom they felt comfortable. Their ideal candidate had to be intelligent, educated, experienced and have a track record of successfully caring for infants and toddlers. Race didn't matter, as long as she spoke articulate English. Maria included an unspoken preference for a Catholic in her private criteria; of that, John didn't care one way or the other. They were beginning to think, in the way first-time nanny employers often do, that no one could meet their criteria. They were, of course, correct, but they refused to recognize it. So the frustrating search went on.

During this time, Renee was a frequent visitor. She wanted to be there simply because she was Maria's best friend. She wanted to help out if she could, and she wanted to keep an eye on how the new mom was coping. She also wanted to keep an eye on Christian. Was he developing normally? Was there anything...anything at all... out of the ordinary? She wondered if she would recognize it, even if there was...And, so far, absolutely nothing. That in itself was comforting, she thought.

On one of those visits, she was accompanied by Paul McCormack. The baby was approaching 5 months and they still had not found a nanny, so it was a natural topic of conversation. Maria couldn't hold back her frustration and growing anxiety. She would **have** to get back to work soon. She was in urgent need of a solution.

Paul said, "You know, I think I might be able to help you." He told her that the Archdiocese had recently been forced, for financial reasons, to consolidate elementary schools. Several excellent lay teachers had to be let go in the process. Really unfortunate. Perhaps not for Maria. Paul had been involved in the closings and was actually trying to help a couple of people find new employment. He told Maria about an elementary teacher named Kathleen Ryan. She was about Maria's age and had raised 3 children of her own. Paul thought she met most of Maria's requirements. She had a degree from Holy Cross, she was bright and articulate, well-respected by the Archdiocese. Unfortunately, she was also redundant. She had spent the last few months working in new born daycare center operated by the Church, so she had the requisite experience on that count. Her role at the center was temporary, so she might consider working for Maria. "I know the fit's not perfect," said Paul, "but maybe you'd like to talk to her and see if you can work something out?"

A few days later, Paul accompanied Mrs. Ryan to the Baptista's home. She met over coffee and tea with Maria and John. It was less an interview than a conversation, sometimes moderated by Father McCormack. It soon became clear that the prospective nanny and the doting parents were comfortable with each other. When Kate was introduced to Christian, she held him and rocked him, smiled at him and talked to him. He responded with a little grin. That was enough for the Baptistas. It would take a little time for them to have full confidence in her, but, no matter: They offered her the job. And that is how Kathleen began her tenure as nanny and significant influence on the life of John Christian Baptista...

CHAPTER 21

M rs. Ryan proved to be a godsend. Maria was inclined, sometimes, to think this was literally true. Kathleen and Maria
bonded quickly. Without being exactly what Maria wanted, she
turned out to be exactly what she needed. The two women com-
municated beautifully together; there was never any doubt about
what was to be done or who would do it in regard to Christian. And
Christian accepted Kate from the beginning as a member of his
family. For ten hours a day, five days a week, she did all the things
a nanny was there to do. She fed him, changed him, bathed him,
rocked him, read to him and sang to him. And she did more: She
quickly came to love this angelic creature. It was easy to do!

Maria and Kate seemed forever on the same page, so there was
never any trouble as they came and went. There was no question
about who was his mom. Maria still nursed him, cared for him in
the evening, slept with him, and prepared him, in the morning, for
his nanny. She devoted weekends almost exclusively to being there
with and for him. She felt thoroughly comfortable spending her
workdays at the Museum. Kate had rapidly become a trusted part
of the family; Maria thought perhaps it was meant to be this way.
Christian apparently felt that way, too. He rarely fussed in Kate's
care, and when he did, he felt comforted by her touch and voice. He
loved his mother in a way that only a baby can; but when mommy
was away - a condition that he simply accepted as normal - his nanny
was a more than satisfactory substitute.

John could sense that his wife was satisfied with Kathleen. He rarely interacted with the nanny because his work usually kept him out of the house at those hours when she was there. On those occasions when he did chat with her, he found her to be the bright, articulate and educated person they expected when they hired her. The important thing to John, however, was that Maria had no anxiety about going to work or being away from their son while he was in Kate's care. Maria's confidence served to reassure him that all was well in the care the nanny provided for Christian. His confidence in his wonderful wife's capabilities as a mother was unquestioned. All was well in the Baptista home....

Out of nowhere, John began to have a series of bad dreams; dreams that scared him and wakened him, but dreams he could not recall. He could consciously get hold of just enough snippets to infer that it was pretty much the same dream repeated again and again. Not knowing was beyond frustrating. He was actually losing sleep and he just couldn't get a handle on what was bothering him. He got out of bed quietly so as not to wake Maria or the baby. After a brief bathroom stop, he found that he was wide awake, so he made his way to the kitchen and placed a pod of hot cocoa in his coffee machine. He sat at the table and drank. The room was illuminated solely by a nightlight; it was the middle of the night, and it was noticeably quiet. He tried to focus, to reflect on what it could be that troubled his repose.

He thought about work. Nothing there. No problems with students or staff, good relations with administration, the lab running efficiently and well. Maria? No, for sure. The baby appeared to be the best thing that ever happened to her, and he loved her. What made her happy worked for him. And he was just as in love with his son as she was. The nanny was working out fine. That made him think of their finances. No, nothing there, either. They were solid. Those notes. Those research notes and observations. They were locked away, secure, but perhaps not in his mind. What if they ever got into the wrong hands? What if they got out? He realized that he was perspiring. Could be that's it. "I've got to talk to Renee," he said to himself as he headed back to bed...hopeful that now he could get some sleep.

Next morning, John called Renee into his office at the lab.

"Who knows about those records, Renee?"

"Just us, John, you and I. I don't even think Maria knows we kept notes."

"There's only one set, right?"

"No, John. We both have partial files. There is no single set."

"Right. Are your materials secure?"

"Locked in my private laboratory safe. I'm the only one with access," replied Renee. "How about yours?"

"The same," he replied.

There was a moment of silence, then John offered: "I guess it's okay." He spoke without real conviction. "Do you think we should get them all together in one place?"

"Actually, John, now that you mention it, perhaps it would be better to have **two** complete sets, just in the event that something unforeseen happens."

This is not where John had expected the discussion to land. "Let's think about it," he said.

That night, he had another frightening dream. This time, though, he remembered, or at least he thought he did: The cat was out of the bag, the horse out of the barn, the genie out of the bottle and the results were horrendous....

The next morning he told Renee to bring her materials to his office. They would combine their notes and lock them in John's safe. From now on there would be only one set and John would have total control. That night he slept better than he had in weeks.

CHAPTER 22

John Christian was approaching his 3rd Birthday. He was a precocious child, bright and articulate. He was not at all gregarious, nor was he shy or withdrawn. He was sociable, but reserved. He was inordinately curious about almost everything, and he demonstrated an unusual degree of comprehension and retention. He had already figured out how to use a phone and an ipad, and, much to her amusement, he would call Maria at the office every day. "Hi, mommy. I love you, mommy. come home soon mommy. bye bye, mommy..." He could count to 20, he could sing the ABC song, and he recognized the letter "C" in his name. He knew his colors - his favorite was red. He had big, brown loving eyes and he had already developed a love of books. He constantly demanded that mommy, or daddy, or Kathleen, read to him.

Kate was only too happy to accommodate Christian's endless appetite for the printed, and, of course, illustrated word. She was a teacher by profession, but also a devout Catholic so she took advantage of this continual opportunity to introduce him not only to the usual children's literature, but to the basic tenets of her - and what she not unreasonably supposed would be his - faith. Christian became well-acquainted with Dr. Seuss (his favorite was "one fish, two fish..."), fairy tales and nursery rhymes. He could recount his favorite stories and was gleeful when the bad guys - the Big Bad Wolf in particular - got their just desserts. With only the slightest prompting he would spin his own unique version of just about any story. He knew alll about Santa Claus and the Easter Bunny, and he had a whole list of books and toys that he expected Santa to bring him when next he came.

It was in that context - Santa Claus, the Easter Bunny and gifts - that Kate began to introduce him to what she believed - and wanted him to grow to believe - was the only true religion. She read him the story of the Nativity and showed him the illustrations of a radiant mother and a holy infant, wrapped in swaddling clothes and lying in a manger. Christian loved the story and the pictures and had her read it again and again. She told him that Jesus was God's son and Mary was his mother. She explained to him that Christmas was Jesus' Birthday. She was careful not to tell him what happened to Jesus, or why he died on the cross. That was too scary and too complicated for a little boy to comprehend. She did tell him that Jesus and Mary were in Heaven with God and he could talk to them by praying. She tried to teach him, "Now I lay me down to sleep," but he wasn't quite ready for it yet, and he thought kneeling down- and standing up, and kneeling down - was a fun game. The idea of bowing his head, clasping his hands and talking to somebody who wasn't there amused him. His amusement, in turn, delighted the educator in er. She didn't force anything on him; on the contrary, she waited for him to be ready. The time would come, she was sure, when he would be, and she would be there to help him understand. Meanwhile, she contented herself with telling him amazing stories: The Great Flood and how God saved Noah and Noah saved all the animals; David and Goliath, and how a boy defeated a giant with God's help; that there was a book called the Bible that told lots of stories like these. She promised to read them to him when he was a little older.

Of course, reading and story telling were not the only things they did all day. They sang songs, played games, drew pictures, watched PBS kids' shows, went to the park, visited the library and did a whole host of things that kids and nannies do. He learned to use the potty, wash his hands, brush his teeth, comb his hair and help get himself dressed. He learned to drink from a cup, gave up nursing in favor of a bink, and gave up the bink in favor of a thumb. Now he no longer needed that thumb! Christian was no longer a toddler. He had become a little boy and he was ready for pre-school. Kathleen thought he was a very special little boy; she had no idea...

On the other hand, Maria did - or at least she thought so. There hadn't been much, just a few isolated incidents that made her wonder, intimate things that only she knew and that she hadn't shared, even with John. Like many mothers, she had suffered mild post partum depression. One day, shortly after he began to talk, she was in the kitchen silently shedding a few tears over nothing worth remembering. Christian was asleep in his crib. She heard him cry out suddenly and call "Mama....mama..." She ran to his side and picked him up. He asked her, quite clearly and distinctly, "Why are you crying?" She was astonished, all the more so when he smiled at her and caressed her cheek with his hand - and, almost magically, the sadness in her disappeared. Had it really happened just that way? She **thought** so, but was it **really** so? Some months later, she was playing with him on the living room floor, waiting for John to get home for the day. He looked up at her and said, "Daddy's hurt." She responded "Yes, honey, Daddy **is** late." A few minutes later, John called. He'd had a minor accident at the lab. He'd cut his hand and he'd had to go to the ER for a couple of stitches. He was fine. He'd be home in a little while. She thought about what Christian had said. Did he say "hurt?" Now that she thought about it, it certainly could have said, "hurt." If he did, how did he know? She shook it off - maybe he **did** say "late," but now she was no so sure...

119

Not too long after that, the dieffenbachia plant in the living room began shedding its leaves. Maria loved that plant. It had been with her for many years, first in her office at the Museum and then, when she was on leave, brought home to stay. It had always had big, magnificently colored green leaves. Now it appeared to be dying. She watered it, fed it, and moved it to a sunnier location, but nothing worked. It was soon reduced to a dry, browning, leafless stalk. Sadly, she carried it over to the back door and set it alongside the trash bin. It was finished. Two year old Christian watched her. He walked over and hugged the plant. It was too much for her. She put it back in the living room. She'd dispose of it some other time, some time when it wouldn't upset her son. This happened on a Sunday afternoon. By the time she came home from work on Monday, she had totally forgotten about the plant, now set aside and abandoned, out of sight on the far side of John's easy chair. A couple of days later, on her way home from work, it re- appeared on her mental to-do list. The trash had to go curbside, and that plant would have to go with it. When she got home and Kate had left for the day, she made her way over to gather up and discard the dieffenbachia. Miraculously, it had fresh new bright green buds at the top of the stem; there were even a couple sprouting from the sides of the otherwise naked brown stalk. How had this happened. She had no idea...or, perhaps she did...

One night, when he was about two and half, Maria was giving him a bath in the tub. A couple of inches of water and an assortment of rubber duckies. She slipped on the wet tile and fell to the floor. She saw stars. The next thing she knew, he was beside her on the floor, peeling back her eyelids. Later, after he was in bed and John was home, she told him about how she had gotten that bump on her head. She didn't tell him about Christian. It was a minor miracle that he had gotten out of the tub without killing himself. It was a minor miracle that he had gotten out of the tub at all.

Maria took great pleasure in sharing the art she so loved with her son. From time to time she would spread open a magnificent volume of highest-quality reproduction renaissance art. She would sit on the floor with Christian and show him the pictures. Maria would point out and name the primary colors. She would describe the people, the animals and various objects that appeared in the pictures. Her usual reward was the little boy's total attention - often for quite a long time. How quickly and easily he learned! His favorite paintings depicted Mary and baby Jesus. He would put his hand on the picture so Maria wouldn't turn the page. He would pat the image with his little hand and proclaim, "Mommy!" Yes, she **was** a mommy. Could she be **his**?

Most recently it was a question he asked. It was bedtime. He was still sleeping with mom and dad - soon he would have his own bed in his very own big boy room. But for now, John and Maria kept him tucked between them at night, warm and snug. She had tucked him in and was singing him a gentle lullaby. His eyes were closed and he was sliding away into whatever dreamland little boys can imagine. Suddenly, he opened his eyes, sat up and said, "Who am I, Mommy?" Just as quickly, he closed his eyes again, lay back on the bed and was sound asleep. She felt goosebumps, then caught herself before she could react. He must have said, "Good night, Mommy." Nevertheless, she recognized in herself a nagging fear and anxiety, lurking just below the surface. And what was that other feeling? Was it hope?

John was proving to be a good father. He was a wonderful role model for his son. He didn't smoke, rarely drank alcohol, was soft-spoken and never used profanity. He loved Maria and Christian and never hesitated to let them know. He hugged them and kissed them and made sure he said, "I love you," at least several times a day. Perhaps just as important, he **listened** to them when they talked. He was an attentive husband and dad. He was also quite matter-of-fact in his approach to life and to his family. Like Maria, he never engaged in baby talk with Christian. They used "grown up" language with him from the beginning. Unlike Maria, whose artistic inclinations carried with them a strong affective element, John was always rational, reasonable and direct. He had no interest in religious dogma and he didn't believe in miracles, so he expected none from his son, even if a genetic link to Jesus was real. He could envision no way to prove such a link, anyway; but he watched his son's development just in case there might be behavioral clues. So far he had observed none; and he really didn't expect to see any. His real focus was on loving his boy and enabling him to grow into an independent man.

CHAPTER 23

By Christian's 5th Birthday, Maria was largely disabused of the idea that her son might be the reincarnate Christ. There had been no revelations, no visionary dreams, nothing prophetic. in short, no indication over the last two years that he was anything but a normal boy. He was unquestionably gifted, especially with intelligence and personality, but otherwise he appeared normal. No visitation by angels, nothing she could attribute to the miraculous, just a little boy demonstrating normal growth and development. She was almost convinced...almost...because she could not forget - could never forget - his genetic background and who he might actually be. But, she consoled herself, did it really matter? He was **her** son; John was his father... and they were a loving, happy family. Perhaps it was just a mother's normal anxiety about the future as she watched her child grow and become ready to meet and face the challenges of the wider world, but she could never quite convince herself it was that alone....

John rarely gave a thought to life before Christian. From a clinical point of view, they had been successful in cloning a perfect little boy from an ancient donor. It was pretty clear to John that at this point - barring something extraordinary - there was little more than normal development to observe and record. But John had stopped thinking clinically quite awhile back. Christian was his little boy and John treasured every minute they spent together. They spent many evening hours, after dinner, at the playground. He taught Chris how to catch and kick a ball, encouraged him to climb and swing high, taught him to pump for himself on the swing. He watched with great pleasure as the little guy's self-confidence blossomed. Many of the other kids who came to the playground were "regulars" and a couple were classmates from Chris' pre-school. They would play together and John enjoyed being a silent observer, as they created their own games - dinosaurs, pirates and aliens were among the favorites. He was amazed at how complicated the "plots" became, how there were always good guys and bad guys and how the good guys (almost) always won. Imagination is an amazing thing, he thought...

There were many other evenings when John sat in his big easy chair with Chris perched on his knee and they read books together, while Maria relaxed on the couch and provided them with an audience. Christian loved books about animals. He was particularly fond of donkeys, cows and sheep, but any animal would do. Dinosaurs were welcome,. too, especially once he'd learned that they all lived and died long ago. "But how do you know about them?", he'd asked. Daddy explained that when they died they left their bones and teeth behind and people have found them and put the pieces back together like a puzzle. Chris liked to do puzzles with daddy, so he understood. "But why did they die, daddy?" "Not all of them did, Chris...some of them turned into birds." Awesome, Chris thought - like magic! Like Cinderella's fairy godmother....

Dr. Seuss books were Christian's favorites. His ABCs always started with Aunt Annie's alligator and ended with a Zizzer Zazer Zuss. He loved the sound of the words and he loved the rhymes. It made it easy to remember things. He took green eggs and ham to heart and was always willing to try something new. But the best part was all the imaginary critters and Chris would always remember "oh the things you can think up, as long as you try." He would carry with him much of what he'd learned from Seuss throughout his life.

John and Chris would build things with blocks on the living room floor. They would configure and reconfigure the track for his wooden train set. Chris learned quickly that there was more than one way to do things. There **were** limits - you could connect the track pieces so they didn't join together at the end and then the train would crash. If you stacked too many blocks they would fall down. But there were lots and lots of combinations that **did** work, and even the ones that didn't were fun to build. Sometimes, knocking down the blocks was the most fun of all. John showed him how to set up a long line of rectangular blocks standing parallel and close together on their ends. If you pushed the first block, one by one, in turn, all the other blocks would fall down. This, too, was fascinating and memorable....

Maria and John together would play games with Christian on the kitchen table. He learned to play Candyland very quickly. At first he would get upset when he drew a card that made him go backwards, but after awhile he understood that that was an important part of the game. He didn't like it, anymore than he liked to lose (which John and Maria made sure he sometimes did), but he accepted it and continued to play.

Maria encouraged Chris to draw and paint. It helped in the development of his small motor skills and in learning about colors and patterns, but that's not really why she did it. She just wanted her son to enjoy what **she** enjoyed and she enjoyed doing it with him. They made painted hand prints on paper; then Maria showed him how to turn those handprints into birds and dinosaurs. He liked to finger paint - the paint felt good on his hands and he could mix the bright primary colors up, but somehow it never made the rainbow he wanted. He created a lot of dark grey "art work" along the way, but whatever he did ended up stuck with a magnet to the refrigerator. It was not until he graduated to tempora paints and brushes that he learned to keep the colors apart **except** when he **wanted** to mix them. He made pink from red and white, purple from red and blue, gray from black and white; but the **real** magic was when he mixed yellow with blue and got **green**. He was delighted.

They made things together out of playdough. Maria would take a lump of the stuff and sculpt it into an animal - a horse or a dinosaur - and he would have to tell her what it was. With a little help and practice, he would make things, too, for her to identify. It was fun and it helped him to understand that he could imagine things and he could make the things he could imagine! They made other things, too. Plaster molds of bugs and butterflies (they took sooo long to dry); all manner of things made of popsicle sticks, pipecleaners, cotton puffs, googly eyes and glue; strings of beads; and lots of other things that let him be creative. Sometimes they made cookies. Chris would help mommy find the recipe. He would put the ingredients into a bowl and help mix them up. Mommy would roll out the dough and he used cookie cutters to make dinosaurs or snowmen or animals and when they were cooked, he would decorate them with icing and colored sugar. Christian loved his time with mommy, partly because he loved to do things with her, but mostly because he just loved her. One day he asked her, "Did Jesus' mommy do fun things with him?" Maria was startled. "I don't know, honey..."

But his nanny did...or at least she believed she did. She believed, too, that it was her duty to share what she knew with Christian. After all, his father and mother were not church-goers; as far as she could tell, they rarely ever spoke about God in this household. True, Father McCormack was the little boy's Godfather, but he was an infrequent visitor, so it was up to her to set Christian on the path to salvation. She read to him from The Children's Bible, showed him the pictures, and explained what the words meant. She would occasionally take him to her parish church, where she introduced him to her priest and let him see the high alter. She explained that this was God's house, a place where lots of good people came to remember Baby Jesus, sing songs and pray. Once she had even arranged to meet Father McCormack at the cathedral. They showed him where he had been baptized and told him that that's how a baby was introduced to God. Standing there, feeling very small, the interior of the cathedral appeared immense to his child's eye. Christian was overwhelmed and silent. He didn't see God. He wondered if God was at home today. If he was, where, exactly, was he hiding?

The nanny did not dwell on religion, but she made sure he was exposed to it as a regular part of her guardianship of the boy. There was nothing surreptitious about what she did. She reported it to the Baptistas, along with all her other activates and observations concerning Chris, on a regular basis. There was a tacit, if not explicit, understanding that they accepted and even appreciated her efforts. In any case, those "other activities" took up almost all the time she spent with the boy...and that time was already limited by his daily attendance at morning pre-school. She helped him learn numbers, letters and how to write his name. She helped him learn to spell and read simple words. They played school together, he the teacher and she the student. They watched one or two selected PBS kids' show on TV most days, and they talked about what Chris learned from watching it. She taught him how to use an ipad in preparation for elementary school and she was amazed at how fast he learned and how adept he became at using it. He knew how to access music and stories and how to actually play electronic games. By the time he was five, she felt, as a professional educator, that he was more than ready to be a full time student. Unfortunately, that meant that her services would no longer be required. She knew she had done a good job, but now it would be up to others - along, of course, with his mom and dad - to enable him to continue to grow so that he could succeed in a competitive world. She had come to love this child and she would surely miss him, but it was time for her to move on as well, and she was ready...

Christian had two Fifth Birthday parties. The first was with his friends at one of those indoor ride and game places that cater just to young kids. All of his friends from school were invited, and all of them attended. Chris was a popular child, if such can be accurately said about a 5 year old. He was self-confident, laid back, and he liked almost everyone. He had whatever it takes to make a kid stand out from his peers, but without displaying a hint of self-importance. It was hard **not** to like him. He and his friends had a wonderful day.

His second party was at home with his small extended "family." Renee Josephson and Paul McCormack came together, still clearly the best of friends. Marty and Matthew showed up bearing gifts, and of course, Nanny was there. There was a big balloon "5" attached to his chair and he sat at the head of the table wearing a cardboard crown. He presided over the mandatory rendition of "Happy Birthday," then, after the cake and candles (he wished that his mommy and daddy would always be there) came the presents. John gave him a learner's microscope with prepared slides. Maria gave him an art kit with paints, crayons, colored pencils and chalk, and a big pad of paper to draw on. When he carefully unwrapped the presents from Marty and Matt he found a couple of popular kids toys that he had asked for. Renee gave him a kaleidoscope, a little brass one of high quality, and Chris was fascinated and delighted. Paul's gift was a dvd called "Star," a children's version of the Christmas story. Finally, Nanny handed him a small, flat box wrapped in Cat In The Hat paper. He thought it would be a book, but when tore off the paper and opened the box he found - Nanny's ipad! He jumped down from his chair, ran over to her and gave her a big hug and kiss. If he'd been a bit older he might have shouted, "You made my day!" But all he did was to look at her face and say "Thank you," and that was enough...

CHAPTER 24

I t was Confirmation Sunday at the Cathedral. Kids were everywhere, the little girls dressed all in white, the boys in suits.
Christian was one of them. He had taken weekly CCD classes with
Father McCormack, who viewed these classes as one aspect of community outreach and healing. The main purpose, of course, was to
prepare the children for this day. But Paul had successfully used his
role as teacher of children to reach out to the parents, to reassure
them that there had been dramatic changes in the Archdiocese and
their children were safe and protected from harm. Paul's quiet, confident manner, and his simple and direct explanation of his own
oversite role won over many sceptics; his warm and easy manner
won over the kids. He found that he actually enjoyed this teaching
role and thought he must find ways to do more of it...

John and Maria were in attendance, John out of a sense of duty
to be there for his son, Maria with a less jaded view. She had been
accompanying Christian to Mass for several months and although
she had experienced no rebirth of religious fervor in herself, she
remembered how important confirmation had been in her young
life. It had made her feel grown up, and that it was something she
had earned, almost like a graduation. She didn't remember if she
thought at all about God, but she did think about her parents and
how proud they were. That made her proud, too. She hoped that
Christian would tap into some of those same feelings today...

In reality, Chris felt none of those things. He was troubled, though if asked he probably would not have known to use that word. Perhaps he would have said, "puzzled," or "confused." He had learned everything that Father McCormack had taught at CCD. He knew about the Church, about priests and the Pope. He knew about sin and salvation. He had learned the Nicean Creed. He knew all of this and he had expected that knowing it would make him somehow different. He'd thought that maybe he would now be able to see or hear God, but as he looked around the Cathedral and listened to the service, what he heard was dressed up people chanting prayers. He didn't see God anywhere and the only answer to the prayers seemed to come from the congregation itself. Where was God if He wasn't here in His house? Maybe He was here, like a ghost. Christian knew what he had learned; he knew what his Godfather believed. But he didn't yet know what to believe himself....

A week or so after Confirmation Sunday, Renee and Paul came by for dinner. Eight year old Christian was full of questions for his Godfather. Chris had recently arrived at the conclusion that Santa Claus and the Easter Bunny were not real. He had begun to be skeptical as his awareness of the world grew. It was just too big and there were just too many kids for Santa to visit them all in one night. When he thought about it some more, he doubted that reindeer could fly or pull a sled through the air. They had no wings. Even if they could, they couldn't bring Santa to every house in the world. And how could Santa actually get down a chimney? How did he get in if there was no chimney? The weight of the evidence gradually built until it brought his belief in Santa crashing down. It hurt to know that Santa was made up. But that couldn't keep him from applying the same logic to the Easter Bunny. He consoled himself with the thought that the presents at Christmas and the candy at Easter were real enough. But then he had another thought. He told his mother that he was pretty sure that Santa wasn't real (perhaps still hoping that she would contradict him, which she did not) and he told her why. Then he asked "Why do grownups pretend he's real? Why do grownups tell kids there IS an Easter Bunny?" Maria was taken by surprise. After a moment's thought, she replied, "It's because we want to give our little kids something fun and magical, something that will make them happy and excited, and that makes grownups happy, too. Once you figure it out, you can be part of the game. You don't have to believe in Santa or the bunny to enjoy the make-believe." Christian, were he somewhat older, might have responded, "That works for me." Instead, he nodded and said, "Oh, okay, mom."

So it came as no great surprise to Maria when Christian asked Paul, "Is God real? I mean, is God like Santa Claus and the Easter Bunny?"

It was Paul's turn to be taken aback. He knew he had done an exceptional job teaching Chris about God and preparing him for confirmation. He had assumed the boy had accepted it all with the faith of a child. "Of course God is real," he replied. "God made us. People made up Santa Claus and the Easter Bunny..."

"But I can see Santa and the Easter Bunny, and they're still not real - just pretend. I can't see God. I look for him every time we're in the Cathedral and he's never there. Is he just pretend?"

John Baptista was mildly amused - he had never really answered that question for himself and now that his son had raised it, he was genuinely curious about how the priest would reply.

Renee, seated alongside Paul, squeezed his hand in hers. She hoped he had a good answer!

Before that reply could be made, Christian abruptly changed the subject.

"Paul, are you married to God? Is that why you don't marry Renee?" A much easier question to answer, at least from a Priest's perspective, thought Paul. Not so easy from the point of view of a man approaching middle age. He simply said, "Yes," and Christian was satisfied.

The very next day, Christian found God....in a manner of speaking. Maria was sitting on the big, comfy couch in the living room with a very large book open before her on the coffee table. She called Chris away from his ipad, patted the seat cushion beside her, and he came over and plopped down . Chris recognized the book. It was "Michelangelo," and it contained exquisite reproductions of all of his work. Chris knew he was a great artist from long ago; mommy had showed him paintings from this book before. Tonight the book was open to a picture that was labeled "The Creation of Adam - Sistine Chapel." Mommy said, "Christian, I know this has been bothering you, so let me introduce you to God..."

Christian had seen this image before, but he'd never dwelt on it. Now he looked carefully. An old man with a gray beard seemed to be floating in the sky. His arm was outstretched and his finger was almost touching the finger of a young man sitting below him to the left. The old man was surrounded, maybe even held up, by a bunch of people who looked like angels. The old man was wearing a robe; the younger man was naked. "Is the old man God, Mom?"

"That's what Michelangelo imagined He looked like, Chris. Nobody really knows what God looks like, but the Bible says God made us in His image, so Michelangelo imagined Him as a powerful older man. You'll have to imagine God for yourself. The important thing is that God is the creator. We create things because God made us like Him. We can imagine Him and create Him in our minds.

You can visit God anytime and He can visit you. Just imagine and He'll be there."

"But Mom, I can imagine lots of things and that doesn't make them real."

"God is real, Chris. Trust me. God is in all of us. You just have to search inside to find Him."

When Christian slipped into bed that night, his brain was still struggling to make sense of what his mother had told him about God. He believed HER but he couldn't quite figure out how to believe IT. He dozed off and drifted into a deep sleep. And as he slept, God came to him. He was not a great light, nor was He an old man. Chris recognized Him immediately. It was someone he already knew, someone whose images filled the Cathedral. It was Jesus. In a soft voice he said," Christian, I am in you and I am with you always. Faith lies within. You can see images of me everywhere, but they are not me. That is why you couldn't see me in the Church. Men made those images, but God made me and God made you. He is within me and I am within you. Always remember, Faith lies within..." In the morning, Chris remembered. He didn't understand it all, but he understood enough. He would never forget. "Faith lies within..." and Christian had found his faith.

CHAPTER 25

The next years were filled with growth and learning for Christian. He was enrolled in a highly respected and notably secular prep school just outside Boston. The school welcomed commuters, and in the early days, his parents arranged their schedules to drive him to school and pick him up. Eventually, like most city kids, he became proficient in the use of public transportation and he was able to make his own way back and forth. He was an outstanding student and when, ultimately, he graduated, he was the valedictorian of his class. His academic interests were broad and the prep school environment gave him the opportunity to explore most of them. He loved the English language, particularly all of its nuances; he read widely and wrote well. He became a gifted public speaker and developed considerable skill as a debater. He thoroughly enjoyed dissecting a proposition and thinking through both the pro and con arguments. History and philosophy ranked high among his intellectual pursuits. He was more than adequate in mathmatics and sciences - in fact, he excelled in some aspects of those disciplines - but they were not central to the man he was becoming. He respected them, understood them, but had no real interest in pursuing them. He dabbled in competitive athletics for a time in the eighth and ninth grades, but although he was a passable soccer player he never got engaged in it and let it go in favor of other activities. He was a good chess player and an outstanding electronic games player. He had many friends, numerous girl friends, but never a real girlfriend. Somewhere along the line he had picked up the nickname, "JC."

When he first arrived at the school he had already developed a genuine curiosity about Christian religion in general and about his own Catholic heritage in particular. At school, this curiosity was cultivated into a serious interest. There was a non-denominational chapel on campus which rarely saw a religious service of any kind. Those students who wished to worship had more than ample options in the surrounding community. It did, however, serve as the location for an ongoing series of conversations - some formal, some informal - about God and religion. The school's intentional purpose was to support the non-denominational and ecumenical sharing of beliefs among students, thereby promoting acceptance of differing views and a fellowship of shared understanding. This goal was largely achieved. But there was an unanticipated result, a spin-off series of more private meetings among small groups of highly interested students to challenge their own and each others' beliefs. Christian was an active participant in these groups, first as an observer and then fully engaged. The meetings lasted only a few months during his Sophomore year, but they provided the immediate foundation for a quest that would occupy him, and at times consume him, for the rest of his life.

While Christian grew and learned, life went on around him. Maria was now an Associate Director at the museum. She was at the top of her profession, internationally recognized for her expertise, and her success was immensely satisfying to her. She felt that life had been good to her - better than good. She had her work, but more importantly she had a life that was centered on and revolved around a loving family. John and Christian were her life. She no longer thought much about how this had happened. It had, and it was wonderful. She felt fulfilled. John's career had been at least as successful as his wife's. He had made several significant discoveries and was confident that his life's work had contributed to a growing and vitally important body of genetic knowledge. His published work was well-respected. He had been rewarded by the University with an appointment as an academic Dean. He loved his wife, was proud of his son, and was approaching middle age not as a crisis, but with complete confidence in himself and his world. Renee, for her part, had changed little. She continued to run her lab and to provide medical support at the fertility clinic. She also continued to see Paul McCormack on a regular basis. He was her steady fellow. They spent a great deal of time together; they enjoyed the theater, dining out, shopping, even an occasional brief vacation to Florida or the Bahamas. They simply enjoyed each other's company. They were the very best of friends and although she thought that under different circumstances they might at least move in together, she knew that would never be possible with Paul. His vocation precluded any such thoughts, and she respected his commitment to holy orders. She thought that perhaps this was for the best, anyway. Their relationship was comfortable for both of them. Sex and marriage might actually threaten all they had together....

Paul, too, had prospered. His community work in the Archdiocese was so successful that the Archbishop called it to the attention of the Holy Father as a model that might be employed in other places. The Pontiff remembered a younger Paul McCormack; he had once done some very personal and very confidential work for the Pope. He was pleased to hear of the Father's good works and in recognition of his achievements, bestowed upon him the title of Monsignor. Paul was, of course, quite pleased, but more for the Holy Father's support of his efforts than for any personal elevation. He believed in his work, and would continue to do it; it was comforting to know that he was at one with John Paul III in this endeavor.

———————

Over the course of his high school years, and then on into college, Christian had many serious conversations with Father McCormack about faith and belief. They started with fairly basic questions and concerns, primarily an extension of Chris' ecumenical discussions at school. As Christian's interest developed and his knowledge grew, those conversations with his Godfather became more and more sophisticated, sometimes bordering on debate. Christian was driven, for reasons unknown to him, to question and try to understand (and possibly even find satisfactory answers to) some very basic questions about man, God and the relationship between them. Monsignor McCormack had long since accepted a set of answers that worked for him. In some sense, he was a professional Christian, so he made an excellent sounding board for his Godson's explorations. And Chris admired and respected Paul, who he knew as a life-long mentor and friend. In short, there was trust, and trust enabled them to risk opening themselves up to one another, to question without fear of sounding foolish, to challenge without attacking. Paul was, of course, motivated by the desire to bring Christian fully into the fold and have him embrace the Roman Catholic Church. He was, however, fully aware of the boy's secular up-bringing, and had accommodated himself to the potential difficulty of the task. He would persevere. There was, after all, one thing in his favor - Christian had often confirmed his belief and faith in God. That was at least a start....

CHAPTER 26

"**D**o you believe everything the Bible says, Paul? My father says it's full of mistakes and contradictions and you can't read it literally. My mother says it's like a work of art. She says you have to look at the whole picture, not just little bits of it. What do **you** think?"

"I think your Mom may be on the right track, Christian. Your Dad makes some good points, but it's the big picture that really matters."

"But what **is** the big picture, Paul? The Old Testament is all about an angry God who only cares about the Jews. The New Testament is all about a loving God who offers everyone a chance to be saved. Can God change his mind?"

"Well, I think the Old Testament was probably written by Jewish Rabbis and prophets. Maybe there were some historians, too. Part of it is real history and part of it is about what they believed. They believed there was only one God, and that they were His chosen people. So God did things and worked miracles to lead them to their Promised Land and as long as they obeyed His commandments, He would intervene in human affairs to take care of them. The books were written **by** Jewish people **for** Jewish people. They recorded God's words and laws as the leaders and prophets received them, and those things and their history is what bound the Jewish people together."

"But what about an angry God, Paul? God did some really awful things. He wiped almost everybody out in the Great Flood. He drowned the Pharaoh's army..."

"The Bible tells us that from the very beginning people disobeyed God's commandments. God wanted to start over, so He destroyed most of what He had created. Noah believed in Jehovah, the one true God, and God chose him to survive the flood and produce the generations that became His chosen people."

"But, Paul, if the Flood was real and Noah and his family were the only survivors, where did all the people come from who weren't Jews? The different races, all over the world? The different religions?"

"Well, son, I guess that's where your Mom has the right idea: You have to keep the big picture in mind. The Flood probably has a real historical basis, but you can't take the Bible story of the Flood literally. It is more about tradition and belief..."

"But if that's not really true, how do you know what Bible stories **are** true and which ones are just stories? What about the creation? What about the Garden of Eden? What about the Ten Commandments?"

"Well, the Ten Commandments are not a story. They are God's directions given directly to Moses and written in stone. They are the foundation of all the things that Jews and Christians believe in common. The creation? Every religion has a creation myth, and the one in the Bible basically says that God created everything and explains why we keep the Sabbath. Who knows how much time a day would have been to God? Does it matter? The story of Adam and Eve is an allegory about good and evil. Did it really happen? **I** don't think so. But that doesn't really matter. What the stories **mean** is what's important."

"So maybe my dad's right, too. You can't always take the Bible literally. But people like the creationists do..."

"People like that are called fundamentalists, Chris. My science background tells me they're wrong. They believe that God created everything exactly as it is in the beginning and that evolution never happened. I can only assume that they think all the evidence for evolution was planted by God to fool us, to test us somehow...that only the Bible story can be true. They're wrong, of course. You don't have to believe that every word of every story in the Bible is literally true to believe the **whole** story it tells. And science doesn't contradict that big picture, just some of the literal interpretations. Science **never** says that God doesn't exist or that He didn't create the universe. And it doesn't say that the meaning of Bible stories is not true. Those things are left to faith and belief, which is where they should be..."

***

"What about the New Testament, Paul? Is it literally true? I have so many questions for you! What about the Virgin Mary? Was she really a virgin?"

"Christian, it's a fundamental tenet of our belief that she was a virgin and God placed Jesus in her womb. It is the first great miracle associated with our Redeemer."

"My father says that in Bible times a virgin birth only meant the birth of a first child, and that Jesus was Mary's first child. Could that be true?"

"There are some things that just have to be taken on faith, Chris. The Christmas Story is one of them, I'm afraid..."

"So **you** believe the story **is** literally true and that Jesus was the son of God and his birth was a miracle?"

"Yes, son, I do. I believe that God can work miracles, that Jesus was His son, and that Jesus could work miracles, too. That Jesus **did** work miracles..."

'What about all the miracles they say were done by saints? Even the Church doesn't believe in **all** of those..."

"I don't really know what I believe about the saints. Maybe some of them had a gift from God and were able to do some miraculous things. Maybe not. What I **do** know is that Jesus could and He did."

"But how do you **know** it's true, Paul? Maybe it's just another story..."

"Son, when I was a boy my mother told me that sometimes you just have to accept things with the faith of a child. For me, this is one of those things..."

Some time later: "Paul, I've been talking to my Dad. He told me some things that I want to run by you..."

"More about the Bible, Christian?"

"Lots more. He said there are a bunch of books called "the Apocrypha" that never made it into the Bible but maybe they should have been included. He told me that some of them are still in the Coptic Bible and that Bible is used by a lot of Christians. I didn't know it, but it turns out there are a lot of Christians called Coptics in Egypt and Africa and it's their Bible."

"Yes, Christian, it's true. The early church had quite a few more testaments and letters than we have today. It became pretty confusing to decide which ones to rely on and which ones not to. In 313, the Emperor Constantine, who had just become a Christian, decided to solve this problem. He called together a Council of Church leaders at Nicea. They decided which books would be included in the Roman Catholic Bible, and that has been the official list ever since."

"So the Bible isn't just God's word. It's what a bunch of 4th century men thought it should be?"

"Not just any bunch, Christian - the recognized leaders of the faith, men who should and **did** know."

"But **how** did they know? Why wasn't the book about Mary Magdalene included? Or the one about Judas?"

"Do you know what the word 'apocrypha' means, Chris? It means writings or statements of dubious authenticity. They were not included because the Bishops didn't believe they were genuine."

"But what if they were, Paul? The Coptics must think they are. My dad says they were kept out because they didn't tell a story the Bishops wanted to hear..."

"Chris, the Bible tells us that Mary Magdalene was a minor character in the life of Jesus. Tradition says she was a prostitute. Any book that claimed that she was something more would have been suspect. And Judas betrayed Jesus. What could his "gospel" tell us?"

"Dad says in the Coptic Bible, Mary Magdalene is a desciple and maybe even one of the leaders. He said she may even have been Jesus' good friend. So why leave her out?"

"I'm sure they had good reasons, Chris. Constantine must have thought so, because he approved their work..."

Later, still: "My dad says there are lots of translation mistakes in the Bible. He said the story of Moses and the parting of the Red Sea is probably wrong."

"Yes, I know that particular one. Some language scholars think the Bible originally said "the reed sea," and this got mistranslated into Latin and then to English as the "Red Sea." Some historian agree. They think Moses would have had to have gone way out of his way to cross the **Red** sea during the Exodus, but he **would** have to have crossed a succession of reedy marshlands. Tidal waters could have withdrawn to let the Israelites cross, and then closed in on

Egyptian chariots which might have gotten stuck in the mud. I suppose it's a possibility..."

"What about Jesus, Paul? The Bible says He was the son of God. Dad says there are plenty of scholars who don't think He ever said that. They think He said He was the Son of Man..."

"Why would He say that, Chris? Doesn't make much sense to me..."

CHAPTER 27

Another time, weeks or months later:

" **M**y Dad says Jesus was probably an Essene..do you think so, Paul?"

"I don't know, Chris. I suppose it's possible."

"I read a lot about the Essenes. They're the ones who wrote the Dead Sea Scrolls."

"Yes, Chris, they were a Jewish sect that lived in their own monastery out in the desert."

"Right. They hid their scrolls in caves when the Roman Army came to put down a Jewish revolt. It seems like the Essenes were wiped out. Anyway, they never came back for the scrolls and now lots of them have been found and some of them have been read. It's pretty exciting stuff."

"How so?" Paul inquired.

"Well, first off, most of their stuff was written a couple of hundred years before Jesus' time. But they were already writing some things that sound like they belong in the New Testament Bible. The best example I found is the Sermon on the Mount. A lot of what's in St. Matthew looks like it comes right from the Essenes. In particular, the Beatitudes are almost certainly Essene. They're in a scroll dated to 175 b.c."

"I suppose it's possible, Chris. But what difference does it make? Maybe it just proves what's in the Bible is true..."

"Well, I think maybe it shows that Jesus was at least familiar with the Essene's writings. Maybe that's where he spent all those "lost years:" with the Essenes. There's a whole Church based on the belief that Jesus was an Essene. John the Baptist was one, too. They say that Jesus was not "of Nazareth," but that he was a "Nazarene." That meant he came from an Essene community at a place called Mount Carmel..."

"Okay...go on...."

"Well, the Essenes believed that a great prophet was going to come. They called him "The Teacher of Righteousness." Maybe that **was** Jesus. Maybe he spent all those lost years when he was growing up living with the Essenes. Maybe he decided to leave the monastery and go out and teach what he had learned there..."

"Or maybe Jesus was the Messiah that the Essenes predicted would come," responded Paul.

"Okay, then," he said, "Let's suppose for a minute that you're correct. Does it really make any difference? Jesus didn't come pre-programmed, did He? He had to learn and grow - unless you think He was born with His entire ministry built in. So perhaps He **did** spend time with the Essenes. Maybe they served as God's vehicle to prepare His Son? In any case, it's certainly one way to explain those missing years."

"But it's more than just an explanation of THAT," Christian exclaimed. In the Old Testament, God is vengeful and the Ten Commandments say things like "an eye for an eye, a tooth for a tooth." In the Sermon on the Mount, Jesus does just the opposite. He says you should love your neighbor and that God is loving and forgiving. Did Jesus learn THAT from the Essenes? Or did God send Him here with that message?"

"I think you're doing a lot of speculating, Chris. But let's assume it's all true. What difference does it make?"

"Well, I can think of one difference," said Christian. "Maybe it explains the big gap between the Old Testament and the New Testament. Maybe the Essenes **were** the bridge between Judaism and Christianity. Maybe what they believed was too Christian for the Jews and too Jewish for the Christians. Maybe that's why they were lost to history for so long..."

———

Later: Christian was alone in his room, books spread across his desk, the computer screen emblazoned with an image of Christ and the bold heading, "Was Jesus REALLY the Messiah?" Chris was reflecting on what he'd read. The article was posted on one of those web sites for sceptics of all colors, and, as many such articles, it made some pretty strong points. The most obvious one was that most Jews, then and now, did not think so: Jesus was a man, perhaps a prophet, certainly not the king of the Jews. Certainly not the leader who would free them from the yoke of Rome. Their Messiah was to be a man of action, more like those who led the revolt in 66-70 A.D. Of course, it didn't work out that way - the Romans crushed the revolt and the Israelites did not regain their homeland for almost 2000 years. No, he agreed, in that sense of the word, Jesus was surely not the Messiah.

The article pointed out that there is no independent evidence, with the exception of a possible mention in Josephus, that Jesus ever lived, and certainly nothing to support the belief that He worked miracles or rose from the dead. He lived at a time when the Roman Empire was in full control of the entire Mediterranean area. The Empire kept records of everything, but there is no record of Jesus **before** His disciples began to proselytize. There is also no Biblical account that actually originates during or immediately after Jesus' lifetime. Plenty of time to invent and embellish before the varied stories - and they do vary in some detail - were written down. The article ended with the observation that the real miracle was that Christianity caught on and, ironically, owed its survival and ultimate triumph in the Western World to a pagan emperor. Constantine the Great believed, and he ordered the citizens of the Empire to follow his lead.

Somewhere in the middle, it raised another interesting question. Did Jesus, assuming He existed at all, actually believe His message was for all mankind and not just for the Jews, because, if so, this was truly remarkable in itself. No one and no religion had ever done that before. The Romans could have imposed their gods on the many peoples they subjugated, but they never did. They really didn't care what the locals believed, and were quite content not to contest those beliefs, so long as they did not stimulate or contribute to uprisings against Roman rule. So, it was asked, did Jesus really intend to be the author of what became Christianity, or was His message really for Jews in Israel? If not, what could possibly have inspired Him to an incredibly advanced **humanist** point of view?

Well, Christian thought, that argument could certainly work both ways...he closed the screen and in the dim light of the blank screen he sat and pondered....

That night, Christian dreamed. Not surprisingly, perhaps, he found himself at a desert place that he knew at once was Qumran, the Essene monastery. He saw a boy, seated at the feet of a great teacher...no, he WAS that boy. He was seated there, learning from the Teacher of Righteousness. God is a loving God. We must love our neighbors as ourselves. Men can choose between good and evil. Salvation is within each of us. Everyone must choose. There will be a Messiah to show the way. YOU are that Messiah - you must learn everything and then you will lead us to a new and glorious promised land...

Christian slept fitfully. When he awoke, he could still hear the now distant voice of The Teacher: YOU are that Messiah. He felt goosebumps, then came fully awake. It was time to go to school.

CHAPTER 28

Sometime later, the running conversation between Paul and Christian continued.

"My mother says the Vatican is the last medieval institution still operating in Western Europe. I guess she means it hasn't changed much in 1000 years. I'm not really sure if she thinks that's a good thing or a bad thing..."

"I can certainly see her point," Paul responded. "The Pope is, in some ways, comparable to a medieval king: The absolute ruler whose authority comes directly from God. He appoints Bishops and Archbishops who rule over large and powerful diocese and they serve as Princes of the Church. The idea of electing a leader, by the way, goes way back into the dark ages and even before. The leaders have an army of knights, in this case the priests. The knights belong to orders. It is a male dominated and male-directed enterprise. The Pontiff actually rules a temporal state, nowadays the Vatican City, but once it was most of Italy. And the Church possesses a wealth of material things. There is a great deal of ritual firmly rooted in the distant past. The Pope's Latin title, Pntificus Maximus, actual pre-dates the middle ages. It goes all the way back to the Roman Empire and was borrowed from the Emperors. So, yes, I suppose your mother has a point..."

"But?" anticipated Christian.

"Actually, Chris, there are a whole lot of buts.

"The first and most important thing is that the Church is there for entirely spiritual reasons - to save men's souls. It is the way to

153

salvation and redemption. It is not bounded by national borders or a time and place. We call it "Catholic" because it's universal. It is the physical representative of Jesus Christ here on Earth.

"The clergy, from the Holy Father all the way to the parish priest, are not employees. They do not work there. They are called to God's service. Nobody hired me, Chris. I'm a volunteer. But not just any volunteer. I've committed my life, and the work of a lifetime, to God and the Church. I am a priest because I truly believe in God, in Jesus and the mission of the Church.

"But," Chris interjected, "the Church has been responsible for a lot of bad things. I think the worst thing is that they killed people who didn't agree with them. The Crusades against the Muslims and against Christian sects. They literally wiped out the Albagensians in France. Then there were all the things Martin Luther said in his 95 Theses: Indulgences to make money for the church and promising salvation to the donors Can you buy salvation, Paul? Authorities to tell you what you had to believe. A Latin Bible that only educated people could read, and in a language used by the church. The Inquisition. And I'm not even talking about the Popes who had children and mistresses or who made Cardinals of their children. I agree that the Church has done lots of good things, but there have been plenty of times when it did the dead opposite of what Jesus said."

"I won't defend the bad things, Chris. I could say they were typical of their times, but I won't, because the Church is timeless, so that's no excuse. No, but what I can say is that it's a human institution, managed by human beings. It can't escape the two millennia of history that have gone into its making, but at its core it is an instrument of God, the direct descendant of Saint Peter, the promulgator of the Christian faith around the world."

"What about orthodoxy and heresey, Paul? Do you really believe that there is only one way to be a Christian, and that's our Church? I mean, do you think heaven and hell are real places and that heretics are damned? What about all the Protestants?"

"Orthodoxy is what you must believe if you are to be a member of the Church, Chris. And yes, we believe that all Protestantism is heretical, but there are parts of it that are not. Individual Protestants are not heretics as long as they believe they are not wrong in their belief. The Church holds that it is better to be a Protestant than a non-believer. And there is always the hope that individual Protestants can be brought into the Church. We believe that heaven and hell are real, and that some Catholics will earn a place in heaven and some in hell, and that the same is true for Protestants."

"So let me get this straight, Paul. If you don't believe the Church is correct you can still be a good Christian, but not a member of the Church? Wow, that's a far cry from the Reformation!"

"Yes, it is, Chris."

"But do all Catholics believe the same things? It's hard for me to believe that. Some of them must just go to Church out of habit. Most of them probably believe the basic stuff about Jesus, the resurrection and salvation. Some of them may even know a lot and are really committed to their faith. But it also seems to me that a lot of Catholics have just dropped out. Educated people in the modern, secular world. It's very hard for the Church to recruit priests in America, and as the population ages and gets more educated, attendance at mass goes down. There have been lots of Church and school closings. Aren't you concerned about relevance?"

"There's too much truth, I'm afraid, in what you're saying, Chris. But the Church is strongest where it is needed most - in the poor, third world countries and among the poor around the world. There are 1.2 billion Roman Catholics in the world, more than half of them in Latin America and Africa. The Church offers them a message of hope, in this life and the next. And the Church is reflecting this in its leadership and direction. The College of Cardinals has about 120 active members. Not all that long ago, it was composed of over 50% Italians. Now it has less than 20% Italians. Instead, it has about 50% from all over Europe, 25% from the Americas and about 25% from Africa and Asia. The Church is responding to and reflecting its truly faithful."

"Where will that take the Church, Paul? Maybe we can talk about that another day..."

"To be honest, Chris, I'm more concerned about YOU. Where do YOU stand?"

A few weeks later.

"Who is God, Paul? My father says God is everything we don't know. God is the ultimate explanation. He says science can tell us what happens and how it happens, it can identify cause and effect and correlations, but it can never really tell us WHY. That's what God does."

"I believe God is the creator of all things, Chris. He gave us free will and we used it badly. He punished humanity, then relented and sent His Son to offer salvation to those who believe in Him. But I believe in the Holy Trinity, as well. Jesus, the Holy Spirit and God Himself co-exist as a single being."

"Did Jesus ever say that, Paul? I don't think so...but never mind, let me ask you this: Where is God? Is he inside or outside of us?"

"That's an easy one, Chris. God is everywhere, omnipresent. He is in us by the grace of faith."

"Then is God a personal God? Does He intervene in human affairs? Does He ever appear to us or talk to us? Does He hear us when we pray?"

"He can be and do all of those things, Chris. But He doesn't reveal it all the time."

"God is omnipotent. If God is all powerful and God is good, then why do good things happen to bad people? Why do good people get hurt or killed by bad people? Why do we have wars? Can God be on everybody's side in a war? Maybe he's on nobody's... ? I have so many questions, Paul. Are heaven and hell real places? Are there angels and devils? Do we have a spirit that lives on after we die? Why do we have to pray to the Holy Mother? What is sin? What about confession and pennance?"

"These are good questions, Chris. I can offer you reasons. There are reasons. But most of them end up in logical paradoxes. What I really believe is that questions like these don't have good answers.. not good human answers, anyway. Because the answers lie in the nature of God and his revelations and they are simply outside the ability of our minds to conceive..."

———

Another time:

"Do you know how many Saints there are, Paul? There are more than 10,000!

"Yes, Chris. Lots of saintly people have lived since Jesus' time. A good number of them were martyrs who died for their faith. Most of them, though, were just exceptional Christians, otherwise ordinary people who lived exemplary lives."

"I thought you had to work miracles to be made a saint?"

"Perhaps not always. Some of them seem to have performed genuine miracles, but most of them probably did things that people in their time thought of as miracles."

"Do you believe in Miracles, Paul?"

"Of course, Chris. Just look around you. Everything you see is a miracle..."

CHAPTER 29

T he time would come, shortly, when Chris would need a miracle of his own. Meanwhile, life went on. Christian graduated from prep school with highest honors and at the top of his class. Although he could have attended any college or university in the country, there was never any doubt which one he would choose: Harvard. His father had done graduate work there, his mother had a number of associations there, and he wanted to stay in Boston. The decisive factor, however, was that Harvard, he believed, was the best place to persue his educational interests. Like many young people his age, Chris was not sure yet what he would do with his life - what profession or career he might ultimately select, whether he would have a family of his own, or even what he hoped to achieve in his lifetime. Unlike some of his high school friends, who had already chosen career paths - medicine, business, and the like - Chris' future was open-ended. He was, perhaps unduly, confident that it would all work out. He knew what he wanted to study, what he was passionate about, and that hadn't changed in some time: Philosophy, history and religion. Maybe, he thought, that one day he would be a teacher.

His father's impressive body of work in the field of genetic research received well-earned recognition. Several of his discoveries had been successfully applied to the production of genetically altered plants and animals. There was even some talk in the field that he might one day be nominated for a Nobel. And there was always talk with his son about the long-term implications of what he was about. John, naturally, never shared what he **had** been about twenty years ago, never let on that he had already made decisions and acted on them, the kinds of decisions that he now talked about **hypothetically** with Chris. Looking at his son now, on the verge of manhood, thinking about the joy he had brought to his parents' lives, John was quite sure he had done the right thing. So John suppressed any lingering feelings of - what? - perhaps fear or anxiety - something he felt but couldn't quite put his finger on. And he talked **hypothetically** with Chris about the impact and the possibilities of genetic research. At the moment, Chris was less concerned about the ethics than he was about the possibilities. Whether or not what could happen should happen was an important issue for him, of course, but right now he was interested in his dad's take on the "could."

"I know it's possible to clone a human being, dad, but what else could you do? Could you make a new human species?"

"Well, son, at the present time we can re-program genes within an organism. We can accentuate certain characteristics that are already in the organism's genetic library, so to speak. Theoretically, we could make smarter, or stronger, or more athletic people, perhaps people resistant to certain diseases. And yes, we can clone complete organisms. But we do not yet have the technology to fundamentally change the dna in a gene to produce predictable and specific results. We're making progress in the lab; we're just not there yet."

"So what kinds of things could you change now?"

"Well, we've identified the location of a number of traits on the genes, the specific content of some of the genetic material, and quite a bit about how to manipulate the dna to activate the traits we want at the right time in embryo development. But we just don't know enough to do things like extend lifespans, eliminate birth defects and the like. Maybe someday..."

"Do you think it will be possible someday?"

"Almost certainly..."

"What about BIG changes, major alterations in the species homo sapiens?"

"Possible. For example, someday we might be able to manufacture a human being capable of living in the atmosphere of another planet. Instead of re-engineering the planet, we would re-engineer the colonists."

"What about behavior, dad? How much of it is based in biology and how much is learned?"

"That's an old question, Chris. Biology sets the boundaries. Maybe it would be possible to change some of those boundaries - or even eliminate them. Maybe we could eliminate anger, for example. No one really knows..."

"How about intelligence...could we use genetics to increase our ability to access all the unused power in our brains?"

"Good question. Maybe. Maybe a lot of things."

"What about spirit, dad? Do you think there's something in us or that we have some kind of essence that's not physical, that's not biological?"

"Honestly, son, I have no idea...if I had to guess, I'd say when our bodies shut down and we die, that's all there is...but I guess the only way to find out for sure is to die and see what happens!"

At about this time, Monsignor McCormack, now approaching his 50th Birthday, received a call from the Papal Nuncio in Washington, D.C. His Holiness had appointed him Auxiliary Bishop and directed that he continue in his current assignment. Paul was first surprised, then profoundly moved by the call. He had never sought position in the Church hierarchy. The Bishop knew this very well, and, yet, he must have had something to do with this. Bishoprics do not simply drop from Rome like leaves from a tree. And this was confirmed a few minutes later when the Bishop himself called to congratulate Paul...and, of course, to tell him of his expanded duties. He would continue doing his educational and community liaison work, but he would now also be responsible for an array of additional activities, including parochial schools, services for the poor and disadvantaged, Catholic Charities, LGBT outreach, and a number of others. Bishop McCormack was about to enter the world of full-time human services administration.

He was proclaimed and invested by the Bishop at a high mass in the Cathedral shortly thereafter. It was a memorable event. The celebrants were all clothed in full regalia and they were a dazzling sight. The service was solemn and simultaneously joyful. At its conclusion, the clergymen and Paul's guests retired to a private room for a small reception. Renee was by his side and couldn't resist a hug and a kiss. The Baptista family was there as well. Christian was naturally pleased for his Godfather's promotion and the recognition of his long and devoted service to the Diocese. He was also a little concerned: Would this change the special relationship he enjoyed with Paul? Christian needn't have worried. Paul McCormack might be a Bishop now, but he would always remain Paul to his friends.

Far off in Rome, John Paul III was sitting alone in the low light of the Papal Apartment. It was late evening and he was doing something he often did of late - reflecting on his long reign and contemplating what was yet to come. He was approaching 80 now, still mentally sharp and in good physical health, but he was slowing down. He tired easily and occasionally napped, but he was still vigorous in public and an effective leader within the Church. Tonight he was visualizing an investiture that was under way in Boston. He remembered Father McCormack as a young man, a man of integrity and commitment, a man he had once entrusted with a personal charge. He tried to imagine what McCormack looked like now and whether he had any notion of what it might have been time

SECOND COMING | CHAPTER 29

for so many years ago. The Pontiff was sure it had been something important, but it had never revealed itself, whatever that self might be. He wondered if it ever would...

Shortly after this, Chris experienced the first real trauma of his life. It began with a text from his father: "Mom in hospital. Not a crisis. Call me." Chris left his books on the reading table and headed for the library lobby, speed dialing dad on the way. John answered on the first ring and, before Chris could say anything, he told him that Maria had apparently had a seizure of some kind at work and they had rushed her to the hospital. She was alert and apparently okay now, so no immediate crisis, but they were going to admit her for testing and observation. John was on his way to the hospital now, driving, and could pick Chris up in about three minutes. A couple of minutes later, Chris was seated next to his dad and they were on their way. They were, or course, anxious and tense. "Anything more, dad?" "Nothing, Chris. Let's jsut get there and we'll see. Whatever it is was sudden. Mom has always been a healthy gal."

When they arrived at the ER, they were greeted with terrible news. It **was** a medical emergency, an emergency of the worst kind. Maria had suffered a second seizure and had lapsed into unconsciousness and they had no idea why. No clue in her medical history. No obvious symptoms. Possibly a stroke, possibly some quick-onset disease, but certainly something affecting her brain. She was in their trauma room and all the necessary tests were being run as they spoke. No prognosis. She was definitely in dangerous territory. She was, however, showing strong vital signs, a positive indication. No visitors for now. Nothing for John and Chris to do but sit and wait...

Maria did not regain consciousness. She had somehow contracted meningitis and she was at serious risk of brain death. They were treating her with a barrage of medications, but her condition was proving unresponsive. The doctors warned John to be ready for an unhappy outcome; persistent vegetative state was a real possibility. John and Chris were encouraged to stay with her, hold her hand, talk to her, let her know they were there for her. That was really all they could do - that, and perhaps pray. John did not believe in prayer, and he wasn't about to beg a higher power for some imagined intervention, even in a crisis like this. He would have to find within himself the strength to cope with his gnawing fear. Chris was not so sure. His mother needed all the help she could get and he wanted desperately to help her. He looked heavenward and whispered, "If you're there, give me a sign." There was none.

Or, perhaps there was. Chris was seated at his mother's bedside. He was zoning out, halfway between wakefulness and sleep when it came to him. He sat up, startled and alert. It was **within him** to do something. He didn't know why; he just knew it was true. Absolutely true. He simply needed to lay his hands on her and will her to be well, and it would be so. As he caressed her forehead, she opened her eyes and smiled at him. He was exhausted by the intensity of his effort and dozed off in the chair beside her. When he woke, he thought he's been dreaming, but it was not a dream. Maria **was** awake and a doctor was telling his father that she had passed the crisis. They could reasonably expect her to recover fully, though that might take a little time. It was nothing short of a minor miracle. Chris smiled and squeezed his mother's hand. She squeezed his hand and smiled. He smiled back....and wondered.....

CHAPTER 30

One Saturday afternoon, a month or so later, Maria was still recuperating, but almost back to being her old self. She was sitting in a comfy chair in the living room browsing through one of her art history books. She had company today: Paul and Renee, John and Christian were all there and at the moment they were engaged in an interesting conversation. Christian had started it by asking the two scientists and the theologian, "How do you know what's true? How do we know what's real? How do we know **anything?**"

"Well, son," John responded, "epistemology is the study of knowledge and it's a huge field of philosophy, so there's no one answer, and certainly no really simple ones. I studied it in graduate school and came to my own conclusions, conclusions that work for me as a scientist."

Paul said, "Part of epistemology is the study of beliefs, how beliefs are justified and which beliefs can be considered as true. That was part of my seminary education, so I can tell you a little about that, Chris."

Renee joined in. "I can think of four or five ways of knowing. You'll know three of them right off, Chris. Idealism is the idea that certain concepts are universal and inborn in human beings and in the nature of things. Plato believed that the concept of a perfect table actually exists, along with a lot of other ideal things and that we inherently know what they are. Then there's rationalism, the use of logic and the mind to figure things out. 'I think, therefore I am.'"

Empiricism is all about experience. You have to experience things to know anything. 'I'm from Missouri. Show me.' Revelation is just what it says: knowledge is revealed to you directly from some mystical source. Finally, there's what's called constructivism. That has to do with passed down and collective knowledge, things you are told are true and that have been believed by lots of people for a long time."

John said, "The one thing all these ways of knowing have in common is called epistemological dualism. That means that the knower is real and what he knows exists in reality outside of him. It is a major assumption. There are other ways of knowing that make other assumptions. For example, Bishop Bekeley of the Anglican Church, believed all things only exist in the mind of God - that nothing has independent reality. In the end, what we think we know is always based on some kind of assumption. But some assumptions are better than others."

"Right," Paul interjected. "Beliefs are like that, too. Some are better than others, depending upon how they are arrived at..."

"Like science," said John. "It's a belief system that combines two different ways of knowing to arrive at the truth. I think its the best way to know things. It combines rational thinking with empirical testing. That's the scientific method: Make a hypothesis then test it in the external world. If the hypothesis is internally consistent and adequate to the reality, and if you can reproduce it again and again, you have a theory and a theory is as close as we can get to the truth. A number of consistent and adequate theories that are consistent and adequate with each other form a web of knowledge. That network of knowledge is subject to change if a more complete knowledge of something comes about and refutes something we thought was true. That's the beauty of science - it's about getting more and better understanding of what's true, so that what we know is always changing, but always based on what we've already established. Why do I think the scientific way of knowing is best? Because it's universal - it works everywhere. And because it's fruitful...it produces real results and improvements in our lives. In fact, we live at a time when science has dramatically changed our lives, and promises to do even more in the future. Just look at medicine, industry, electronics, flight, nuclear power - the list is endless..."

"But science can't help us understand God," said Paul. "God is not an empirical thing to be measured or a rational thing to be rationalized. Science is not the cause, it is the consequence. It is bound by the limits of the human mind and what it is capable of. God is spiritual and he is not subject to the laws of science. In that sense, belief and faith are as much fact as any scientific theory..."

"Wait a minute," said Chris. "Science **can** prove beliefs are wrong. Think about Copernicus. People believed that everything in the heavens revolved around the Earth because God had made man the center of the universe. Then it became clear that the Earth revolves around the sun and there are a bunch of other planets and whole galaxies and our Milky Way is really a long, long way from the center of things. So the belief was wrong."

"True," said Paul. "But some beliefs have been tested and proven true. And for all the testable beliefs, there are just as many that cannot be tested at all. We can't run an experiment to find out if the Trinity is real, or if Jesus was raised from the dead. These beliefs are founded in history and passed down as cultural knowledge and experience, but many of them are rooted in revelations. And just like science, when enough of these beliefs come together, they form a faith. This is the basis of Christianity..."

"So let me get this straight," reflected Chris, "Scientific truths are subject to change, but the scientific method, a belief system, is not because when it gets things right it produces useful results and enables man to use his brain to change the world. Belief systems may or may not be true, but only some of them are subject to verification. The ones that are beyond science's ability to test fall into the realm of faith. God, and many of the beliefs we associate with God, fall into that category. I think I understand, but I'm not sure that really answers my question...maybe it just can't be answered at all...."

A few weeks later, Chris stopped by Paul's office for a visit. He was housed in a building that had once been a convent but which now served as administrative headquarters for a variety of Diocesean activities. Paul's secretary welcomed him and asked him to have a seat. She buzzed the Bishop and let him know he had a visitor. After a moment, Paul stepped through a doorway at the back of the room, greeted Chris warmly and invited him in. Paul's office was modest and it was sparsely furnished, but there were two large leather chairs set on either side of a small coffee table. Paul motioned to one and Chris sat down; Paul settled easily into the other. After a few minutes of small talk, mostly about Maria's apparent full recovery, Paul initiated the more serious conversation.

"So you want to talk about revelations, Chris?"

"Right. After we all talked about ways of knowing, I was really curious about it, so I started digging. I found lots of examples, like the prophets in the Bible, Mary and the angel, Constantine and the Cross, right up to modern times and the children at Fatima. And revelations aren't restricted to religion. The best example I found was Edgar Cayce, who lived in Virginia in the mid-1900s and made all kinds of predictions based on things revealed to him by some mystical process. I'd like to talk more about Fatima and the three prophecies, because they really caught my attention. But right now what I want to talk about is the Book of Revelations and I **know** you're the best possible resource!"

"Sometimes you give me too much credit, Chris! I'm not an expert on Revelations, but I can summarize it in a minute. It is the last Book of the Canonical Bible and its title is from the Greek Apocalypse, which means to reveal divine mysteries. It was written by a man who called himself John of Patmos. It has three parts. First, it is a letter, or epistle, to early Christian churches in Asia; second - and this is the bulk of the book - a large number of extraordinary visions; and, finally, several prophecies. It is basically a story of good versus evil and the ultimate triumph of good when Jesus returns."

"Remember we were talking about how you know that revelations are true? Well, most of the visions in The Apocalypse are virtually impossible to figure out. Some of it, okay. The Four Horsemen - War, Famine, Plague and Death. The Beast. The mystical numbers 777 for Good and 666 for Evil. But most of the rest of it has been interpreted about a million different ways. If you can't even agree on what it means, how can we decide if it's true?"

Paul responded. "Perhaps the best way to interpret it is that it's allegorical. I certainly agree with you, though, that there are many, many interpretations. Just for one, he talks about Christ coming to rule on Earth for 1000 years. But we believe that Jesus could never be an earthly king, so he must be talking about an allegorical kingdom of peace on earth..."

"You said that one way to judge the truth of a revelation or a belief was its pedigree. What is its history, what is its foundation? Well, I have to say that I think the whole business of Revelations is on shaky ground. It's not at all clear who wrote it - certainly not one of the Apostles. It has so many references to the Old Testament that many scholars think of it as more Jewish than Christian. The whole concept of direct revelations from God is Old Testament. And yes, there are plenty of scholars who think the whole Book is an allegory. Some people think the revelations are real and they're still to come. Others think most of them have already happened. And a few historians think it makes interesting reading, but that it can actually only be interpreted in its historical context."

"Well, Chris, the context is pretty well understood. It was 1st century Christian, meant to exhort the early churches to keep their unique identity and not become allied with various non-Christian practices. It was included in the Cannons at Nicea probably because the visions came from Christ and foretold His second coming."

"But it's not that simple, Paul. It was disputed from the beginning. It was the last Book accepted into the Bible. At the time, Eusebius wrote that there was real ambivalence about it, that there were reasons for accepting it and reasons for rejecting it. Its authorship was in question and there was a belief that most of it was actually written before Jesus and not about Him. Over the next couple of hundred years, different Church Synods included or excluded it. But by the mid 5th century, its inclusion was widely accepted. Later on, though, the Protestant Reformation was very critical of it. Martin Luther was quoted as saying that Revelations is "neither apostolic nor prophetic." John Calvin wrote a treatise on every book of the New Testament **except** Revelations, so it's clear that he didn't think much of it..."

"I can't argue with you, Chris. As far as I know, everything you're saying is true. For me, as a Catholic and a priest, the Book is part of the Cannon. Within a broad scope I can interpret it as I will, and I interpret it allegorically. But you're right to question beliefs founded on interpretations of what you see as questionable sources..."

"Another thing, Paul. An important thing. Revelations is even suspect when it prophesizes the second coming of Christ. The early Christians thought Jesus' return was imminent. To forecast for thousands of years in the future and cast it as a literal kingdom on earth was totally inconsistent with beliefs at the time. Has the second coming actually been revealed?"

They talked on for some time, parted with an embrace, and Chris headed for home. He wondered if Jesus **would** return and whether it would be like it was described in Revelations. He couldn't answer the first question, but he was pretty sure that John of Patmos got it wrong. It would not be too long before Chris had much more srious and personal revelations to deal with.

CHAPTER 31

I t was afternoon. Chris was at school, in the library, concentrating, as he tapped the computer's keyboard. He was working on an important academic requirement. He wrote:

"DRAFT SENIOR THESIS PROPOSAL prepared by j.c. baptista

What Would Jesus Do?

If Jesus Christ were to return tomorrow, what would He do? How and where would He make Himself known? Would He make Himself known? Would He be recognized? Would He come pre-equipped to comprehend the modern world? If not, what would He think of the diversity, the technology the numerous religions and the secularity of the Western world? Would He come as a God or as a man, as a teacher or a leader? What would He think of the various branches of Christian faith and theology? Would He confront or tolerate beliefs that He found inconsistent with His teachings? Would He reward the good and punish the evil? How would He determine who belonged in which group? How would His life in a small, ancient Jewish community relate to the 21st century? How would His teachings, based in Jewish law and tradition, apply? Could He, or should He, adapt or would He expect the world to conform to His vision. Would He work miracles? Would He confirm the Biblical accounts of His life? Would He show the marks of crucifixion? Would He recognize the Roman Catholic Church and its billion-plus followers as the true faith? Would He recognize the Pope as a direct descendant of Saint Peter, or that He had given Saint Peter the keys to the kingdom of heaven? What would He say about heaven? About spirit? About God and the Trinity? What would He say about people of other faiths - Muslims or Buddhists for example? Would He make the world better or be overwhelmed by it? Would His message change if He had been brought up in a modern American city instead of in the ancient Middle East?

Written from the perspective of a nominal Catholic brought up in a scientific household. Student of both. And the answers also have to reflect this dichotomy...if Jesus was (or is) God, or if He was (is) not. My personal bias is to argue that He was not God, simply a representative of God, and actually a great humanist. But if this is so, how could He return? Let us postulate that somehow He does, perhaps by some divine intervention, perhaps by the hand of man, in any case as a messenger. If, on the other hand, He **is** divine, His return is no problem, but it is potentially much more problematic. Human beings are, after all, bound by laws of nature and physics, so there is a limited, if very broad range of possible thoughts and behaviors. The Divine must remain largely outside the scope of human understanding, bound up in mysticism, known only to the degree that the divinity chooses to reveal itself. So it is possible to say that if Jesus was (is) a man, we can strive to understand Him rationally and empirically - that is to say, from a scientific and humanistic perspective. If he was (is) divine, our answers will become more speculative and they will bring belief and faith into full play.

Much of this paper reflects a series of conversations with my father, Dr. John Baptista, a noted geneticist and scientific researcher; and Auxiliary Bishop Paul McCormack of the Boston Diocese. It is backed by a considerable amount of academic research done over a period of several years and to be fully annotated in the final draft. The topic was chosen because it addresses significant philosophical and epistemological issues, and because it has been a long-standing

- almost life-long - personal interest. The paper provides me with an opportunity to pull my thoughts together and present them in an organized fashion. I believe it will appropriately meet all the requirements for an acceptable senior thesis."

Chris logged off and left the library.

___

Outside, on the Quad, there was always something going on. Today, among other things, a couple of graduate students were collecting saliva samples and donor background information as part of a social psychology project. They were interested in exploring correlations between self-reported racial and ethnic background, actual genetic background, and a couple of behavioral markers. Chris was intrigued and he took a few minutes to fill out their survey and provide a sample. The carrot for participants was that the project would provide each individual with their own genetic profile and interpretation, should they so desire. Chris checked off the box and provided his email address. He went on about his day and thought nothing more of it.

___

Across town, someone else was concerned about genetic markers. Renee Josephson had been troubled for some time - increasingly so lately - about Christian. It was not so much that she felt guilt over the role she had played, with John and Maria, in bringing him into the world. It was more a growing anxiety about the consequences should he ever find out. She was also aware that they knew nothing about the medical history of the genetic donor and how that might be reflected in Chris' health. Finally, there were the potentially unresolved biological consequences of the cloning process - the very real potential for organ failue which, to date, had not manifested itself and - hope to God - never would. Renee felt more and more that she had to unburden herself, that she needed to **do** something, but she had no idea what that something should be. Perhaps she could talk to Maria and John, but she wasn't sure she wanted to risk it. They had clearly suppressed any memory or concern about their son's birth once it had become clear that he was in no immediate danger from the cloning. From their perspective, Chris had grown to be a healthy young man and there was no need to revisit old anxieties. No, Renee thought, that's not the way to go. There has to be a better way...

Coincidentally, at about this same time, and unbeknownst to Renee, John Baptista was drawn to his office safe by concern over Chris. He had repressed, but he had not forgotten. Should he destroy his research records so there would be no chance that Chris could ever know? Should he continue to preserve genetic material he had used? Could he possibly use some of that material to ferret out potential health problems for Chris? What value was there in keeping the records - records that would likely never be published and probably never should be? Why not just destroy them? He hesitated, then put them back and closed the safe...he couldn't help but think that a decision put off is a decision made...

CHAPTER 32

R enee **had** decided. She was going to do something she had not
done in a very long time. She was going to make a confession.
To a priest. In a Confessional. It was a decision not easily taken,
one she had genuinely struggled with. She would share what she
had done not in hope of absolution or salvation, but in the expectation of getting some guidance about what she should do **now**. It
could be done in absolute confidence: Only she and her confessor
would know and he would be bound by the rules of his vocation
to keep her secrets. She could trust him, of that she was absolutely
sure. It might take a bit of arranging, but she was pretty certain it
could be done.

Or, perhaps not. When she broached the subject with Paul over
lunch that afternoon, he was sympathetic but reluctant. Renee had
been a lapsed Catholic for most of her adult life, certainly for as long
as Paul had known her. What was her sudden urgency to confess?
And, more importantly, why would she want to confess to **him**?
They had been the closest of friends for almost 20 years, and he was
inherently uncomfortable with the idea of hearing her secrets, especially ones that she had kept out of their personal relationship for so
long. There was no restriction preventing her from walking into any
church at any time and offering her confession quite anonymously.
What was her urgency and why him?

Renee was willing to share just enough to get him to take her
seriously. She wanted him because she thought he was uniquely

qualified to understand what she needed to say. He was a priest and he had a scientific background. She trusted his judgement. He was her friend and she couldn't tell him what she wanted to **as her friend**, because she didn't know what he might do with the information or how it might burden him personally, but she **could** entrust it to him in his role as confessor. She needed him to know and she wanted his advice, but it could only be via the confessional. And one final thing: In a peripheral sort of way, Paul was involved, so he deserved to know and it was appropriate for him to hear it from her.

Paul had no real idea of what she was alluding to, but she was insistent and persistent and eventually his resistance was overcome. Had it been anyone but Renee he would have said no. But it was Renee. And he couldn't deny that his curiosity had been roused. What was it that she found so troubling, and how could he help her? He had loved her for a long time and, within the bounds of his calling, he would do most anything for her. In that light, hearing her confession really didn't seem too much to ask...

The next morning, Renee sat opposite Auxiliary Bishop McCormack in a confessional booth at the Cathedral complex. "Forgive me Father, for I have sinned. I have lied by omission; I have conspired to play God; and I am deeply troubled by the result." She told him that John, Maria and she had taken genetic material from the Sudarium and used it to clone a human being; that Maria carried the fetus to term under Renee's care, and that John Christian was that baby. Paul was stunned at this revelation, but kept his astonishment entirely to himself. He instantly realized, of course, his relationship to the initiation of these events and how closely he had become intertwined with the principals - especially Renee and Christian - over the years. And he anticipated what she would say next: That she had never been able to discuss this with anyone other than John and Maria, that Christian was totally unaware of it, and that she felt that John and Maria had suppressed the past and were unwilling to talk about it...or, at least, that she, Renee, was unwilling to risk opening the subject with them. She said she thought Chris needed to know, but she wasn't really sure. And she added one after-thought, something she had not planned to say, something that had not come to mind in many years: What if they had cloned Jesus? She had seen no evidence of it, but what if they had? "So you see, Father, why I had to have you as my confessor. What am I to do?"

Paul was silent, reflecting, thinking carefully before he spoke. Finally he said, "You were right to come to me. I can absolve you of your sins, and I do. But you must atone for them. You must discuss this with Maria and John and the three of you must determine what is best for Christian. What are the consequences if he is told? What if he is not told? These are not easy questions and there is no right answer, but you came here knowing that it is not right the way it is now. I will be happy to help you, as a priest and as a friend, if you decide to allow me in. You will have to determine if that is your decision or a decision to be made by the three of you. Or you may choose not to share this with me outside of the confessional and that will be the end of it. Even given the extraordinary circumstances, I will not act or intervene on my own without your specific permission. Let me leave you with one thought: Perhaps the three of you have unwittingly done God's work and it is time (that phrase resonated with McCormack) for a revelation."

The session was over. Renee left the confessional and walked away without pausing to look for or await Paul. She had a great deal to think about. One thing was certain, however: She had sought his advice, he had given it and she would follow it. She would talk with John and Maria, and she would do it soon...

At this very same time, Christian received a text. He was baffled. The dna results were in and according to the graduate student charged with their dissemination, he was virtually 100% Middle Eastern. This result was totally inconsistent with his self-identification as being of Italian and Cape Verdean heritage. It made no sense to Chris. It had to be wrong. He'd have to check in with the project people and have them do it over. Or, maybe it just wasn't worth the bother...

CHAPTER 33

Over dinner that evening, in the course of conversation about the day, Chris mentioned his bizarre dna results. He chuckled about the absurdity of it and said he wasn't sure if he'd go back to tell the grad students. He supposed he owed it to them as a fellow student - to help them clean up their data and get it right. Maybe he'd just text them. No big deal, really; actually kind of funny. How could a kid Boston born-and-bred with Italian and Portuguese parents have Middle Eastern and North African roots? "Maybe you guys should be tested," he said jokingly to his parents, "Maybe you're really Scandinavian and Irish!" To all appearances, the conversation moved on to other topics, but it had stopped cold in John's mind and Maria's heart. They didn't need to risk eye contact to share their shock and anxiety.

As Maria began to clear the dishes from he table, the phone rang. It was Renee. Maria's immediate thought was whether she should tell Renee what had just happened at dinner. The question was pre-empted, however, by something in Renee's voice, a stress and hesitancy that stuck her immediately as completely out of character for her friend of so many years. Something was wrong and she felt a small ball of tension tightening in her stomach. Was Renee in trouble? Had something happened to Paul? No, responded Renee, it was none of those things. She was fine and Paul was okay, too. Maria felt a momentary sense of relief, but then came the bombshell. Renee wanted to meet with her and John to talk about Christian.

She explained succinctly that she had been troubled for some time about Chris, that she'd sought advice in the confessional, and that advice was to meet with the people who shared her secret and talk it out. The priest thought they owed it to Chris to tell him all. She did not mention that Paul was the priest, or that he had used the word "atonement."

Maria felt chills for the second time in less than half an hour. She wanted to shut it all out. She wanted to cry. She wanted to resist. Maybe Chris would not follow up on his dna results, maybe he'd just laugh them off and let it go at that. Possible, she thought. But Renee, that was an entirely different story. Why hadn't Renee **ever** said anything? Why now? What would happen if she said no to Renee? Would she talk to John? What would **he** say? Would Renee break their trust of silence and go to Christian on her own? She desperately wanted to say no, and hope that it all went away. But she knew it wouldn't. It had always been inevitable. Nevertheless, as she thought about it, real terror was welling up in her breast. What would this mean to her perfect life and more important what would this mean to her son. God, she loved that boy, and now...All this went through her mind in seconds, while Renee continued to talk. Then she heard herself saying, "Yes, okay, we'll meet." She stood there looking emptily at the phone for a few moments after Renee had hung up. It was all too overwhelming. She tried to think, to concentrate, but she drew a blank...

The three of them met the next day at John's Office. To say the least, John was ambivalent about the meeting. He wanted to protect his son. He wanted to protect his wonderful relationship with his son. He was simply not sure how best to do it, now that the cat appeared to be coming out of the bag. Unlike Maria, John was pretty sure that Christian **would** follow up on those dna results and he and his wife would have some serious explaining to do in any event. But Renee?...He was a little disappointed in her. If the dna testing wasn't an issue, he would probably have tried to talk her out of this meeting. They had kept this secret to themselves for so many years. It was so far in the past that if it weren't for Christian himself, the whole thing might have been tucked away in the safe and forgotten. Now, however, when he was forced to face up to it, he had to admit that he, himself, had not forgotten. He had always worried just a little about that research in his safe and what to do with it. He had always been concerned that someday it might come out. He had long ago analyzed the boy's dna for any indication of inheritable disease or predisposition; he was relieved to have found nothing significant. That and carefully monitoring the boy's health and development had been enough. But was it? He had, he reminded himself, recently decided not to decide. It appeared that that was no longer an option.

When they were seated, Renee began the meeting with an explanation of why she had never before brought this subject up directly with John and Maria. She was clearly uncomfortable, but they knew her more than well enough to recognize that she was sincere when she explained that she had never wanted to discomfort or upset them over something that seemed to be ancient history. She went on to reiterate what she had told Paul: That she was not so deeply concerned with what they had done as with the fact that they had hidden it all these years from Christian, and what the consequences of so doing might ultimately be. He had grown to adulthood, and he had a right to know. She recognized that this, in itself, was a risky proposition for all concerned, but she was convinced that it had to be done. The three of them were getting older, the secret might be lost, and Christian, unaware, might suffer dramatic consequences. She would not tell Christian - or anyone else - on her own, so she had decided to ask for this meeting to see if the three of them could agree on what to do.

John and Maria listened quietly. When Renee paused for a response, John spoke first. There was a tired acceptance in his voice.

"You may be right, Renee. A couple of days ago, I might have argued the point with you. But there's been a rather unexpected development that changed my mind. Chris has had a dna test and it has revealed that he is clearly not our biological son. It was the result of a project at school, and his first response was to laugh it off. But I'm quite sure he'll follow up and discover that the test was accurate, and that will force us to deal with the same problem you have raised."

Maria was already on the verge of tears. She dreaded coming to this meeting. She had hoped that John, when she told him about Renee's call, would just say no and that would be the end of it. But, instead, he had called Renee, spoken to her for a few minutes, and agreed to meet. Maria didn't feel betrayed, but she did feel very much alone. She had convinced herself that the dna problem would turn out to be nothing. To hear John say he was quite certain that it would have to be dealt with was a blow. And then to hear him say he agreed with Renee that they would have to **do** something was more than she could take. They should let it lie, cover it up, do whatever was necessary to keep things as they had always been. They should do it for Christian's sake and for their own. She was filled with dread and a sense of impending disaster. Her mother's intuition said not to do this, but she knew she had no choice but to go along with it. She began to cry.

The question now was no longer whether to do something, but what to do and when. Their preference was to wait the couple of months until Christian graduated from Harvard. That way, no matter how he reacted, it would not interfere with his education. Whether they could wait that long, however, would really be dictated by the dna testing. If he pursued the matter and got confirmation that the test was correct, they would have to deal with it at once. When was the easy part. Exactly what to do was much more problematic. Who should tell him? How? and how much would they share? Certainly, the essential fact that he had been cloned. More than that? Maybe, maybe not. They were just not prepared to answer those questions at this time. John and Renee agreed to think about it and get together again in a couple of days. Maria was not convinced, but she had pulled herself together and she nodded her agreement. She had no choice but to go along for the ride...

CHAPTER 34

Meanwhile, Chris's academic advisor had approved his Senior Thesis Proposal in principle. They had met in the Professor's office to discuss it. Dr.Johnson told Chris that he thought it was quite an interesting approach to some very significant philosophical questions, but, that as proposed it seemed a bit broad to handle in a single paper. It would serve him well to narrow it down, he said, perhaps just to focus on a few of the issues raised. Two modes of thought were identified as ways of knowing. Perhaps he could concentrate on what differentiates scientific systems from belief systems, and how those differences might play out in regard to just a few of the questions Chris' proposal raised. Chis felt relieved that his concept was acceptable, and was perfectly satisfied to follow Johnson's advice. It would certainly make the project more manageable. He agreed to make revisions and submit them within a few days. He would have no trouble with the science and belief part, but he would have to decide what questions were in or out. Which ones were most important? Which ones loaned themselves readily to the themes of knowledge and belief? That would take a little more doing...

Chris was at the library now. He had just come across a reference to a 20th century Beat poet, a man named Kenneth Patchen. He had never heard of Patchen, but he was taken by the quote in the essay he was reading. "Born as a veritable living prince, with small, pink rectangular feet and a disposition to hair, I stand now and wonder at the disappearance of all things holy from this once so promising land; and it does not much surprise me to be told that at 7 tomorrow morning an angel of the lord will come and clean up people's messes for them. Because if he is. And he does. He'd be more apt to rub their bloody snouts in it." Powerful stuff! Is that what would happen? Could this citation serve as a lynch pin for his own analysis? He'd have to think about it...but, on the surface, at least, it set up the potential difference between the response of a loving god as opposed to the visceral reaction of a man.

He shut down his computer for the day and as he was leaving the library he noticed one of the graduate students who had taken his dna. He was seated at a reading table. Chris walked over and introduced himself and explained his problem with the dna results. The grad student seemed surprised. He told Chris that they'd been conducting tests for some time and this was the first time he'd heard of a possible error. He said he'd be happy to look into it, but perhaps it would be easier to simply re-test. He didn't have a kit with him at the moment, but he told Chris to drop by the library the following afternoon and he would be there to take a new sample. Chris thanked him, said he'd see him then, and left for home. The next day he kept the appointment for another swab.

───────────

That same afternoon John, Maria and Renee met again in John's office. He told Renee something that Maria already knew: Chris was, in fact, taking a dna re-test at that very moment. The results could come back anytime, probably within a couple of weeks. Whatever they decided to do, they would have to act quickly. Renee's response was totally unexpected.

"Before we get too deeply into this, there's something I really have to tell you. The priest who heard my confession, the one who offered me advice...it was Bishop McCormack."

"Oh, my God!" Maria moaned.

"That could certainly complicate things," said John. "What will **he** do, Renee?"

"Nothing, absolutely nothing, John. He heard my confession in absolute confidence and he will say or do **nothing** - unless we tell him it's okay. And that's why I'm sharing this with you. I think he should be part of this. He was there at the beginning and he's so close to Christian. He's our friend and we can trust him. I actually think we **need** him to help us."

Maria looked at John and said, with some relief, "I think she's right, John. Chris might be really angry with us, but Paul really had nothing to do with it and he never knew about it. He **is** Chris' friend and he's always been a mentor and sounding board for him. He could be the one Chris can count on if he doesn't feel he can count on us. If Chris goes over the edge, Paul could be the bridge back..."

"Okay," said John, "But is Paul **willing** to do it? This is some pretty heavy stuff for a priest..."

"I think he will, John," Renee replied. "I think he cares more about Chris than he does about making any moral judgements. With your permission, I'll ask him...

"Okay, but only if he agrees to keep the whole business confidential..."

"Yes, John. I think he will...."

She fished her phone out of her purse and called Paul. He didn't answer, so she left a message: "How about dinner tonight? Call me."

For the time being, the three of them had done what they could. They agreed to meet again tomorrow and went their separate ways... each of them thinking about the task ahead.

Paul McCormack was anxious to help. He agreed immediately when he met Renee that evening. He told her that he wasn't sure how Chris would respond in the long haul, but he was pretty certain that his initial reaction would be traumatic. Under the circumstances, what else could it be? Like most good priests would, he had gotten over his initial shock in the confessional, and now he was focused only on the consequences. Yes, first you had to own the sin, and they had done that. Then atonement. Only after that could you really find absolution and redemption. He had a part to play in the atonement and he would play it. He would be there primarily for Christian, but also for supporting his friends. He expected that they would all get through this, even though the cost might prove to be high. Atonement did not come easily. The absolution and redemption would be up to a higher power....

The four of them met in John's office the next day. After Paul made the appropriate assurances and commitments, they got down to business. The plan they agreed upon was simple. They would gather in the Baptista's living room and be there when Chris returned from school. John would acknowledge the accuracy of the dna testing and tell Chris they owed him an explanation. He would say that three of them, himself, Maria and Renee, had been involved in a deception of sorts, one that they had thought was for Chris' own good. Now they had changed their minds. Chris was mature enough to know the truth, for better or worse. Paul had never known about the deception until now. He was there to reveal the truth in an unambiguous and unemotional way, and because he was their friend and Chris' Godfather. They would not do this for a least a couple of days, to give Paul a chance to grapple with what he would actually say. But they agreed that they would do it soon. The dna test clock was ticking. They left the meeting each with their own thoughts percolating. Maria imagined disaster. John thought that there would be some difficult days ahead, but things would work out in the end. Renee felt a sense of relief that this would finally be done. And Paul? He couldn't keep himself from thinking that the best laid plans of mice and men......

CHAPTER 35

C hris spent a normal day at the library reviewing research materials for his thesis. He was beginning to feel a bit of time pressure - he only had about 8 weeks left to finish up and submit it. He remained confident that he'd get it done. Proceeding on Dr. Johnson's advice, he had simplified it considerably. He had completed drafts of the science and belief sections and was quite satisfied with them. Some things were knowable by one system, some by the other, and sometimes, under the right circumstances, they could confirm each other. In some sense science was a belief system, but it had the advantage of testability. You could use the five senses and instruments that extended them to see if the natural world confirmed what your rational mind conceived. In this way, science could sometimes disprove a belief, but if that belief was part of a larger community of beliefs, the scientific evidence would likely be subsumed or dismissed. Belief systems were a sort of self-fulfilling prophecy -if you believed any of it, you believed most or all of it and you would perceive things accordingly. And, of course, many very significant beliefs could never be "proven" or "disproven:" They existed as revealed or handed down concepts in the minds of the believers, reinforced by rules and institutions.

This is as far as Chris had gone. He was now working on the consequence of belief or science in the guise of a second coming of Christ. He was inching toward a radical conclusion. Perhaps Jesus as the Son of God and Jesus as the Son of Man would not, in many ways, be so different. In fact, the more he thought about it the more convinced he became. The main difference would be the Divinity of God as opposed to, for want of a better word, the divinity of man. The idea that God was the reason to do good or fear doing evil, as opposed to the judgement of men. The notion of miracles, divine intervention and heaven and hell as opposed to the rules of nature, evolution and the laws of nations. But strip away much of the extraneous baggage - if such important issues can be so cavalierly dismissed - the views of science and humanism are not so different from those of Christians. Yes, he thought, in many ways they coincide. Whether man made God or God made man, the two concepts are ultimately inseparable. No, not quite: What actually separates them are the belief systems that have grown up around them. He shook his head. He was beginning to think in circles. Time for a break. He shut down the computer and headed for home.

He hadn't gone far when his phone pinged. Email. He opened the message. "dna confirmed," was all it said. What the hell? What had been funny had suddenly turned dead serious. How the hell could he be Middle Eastern? If the test was right - and now he had to believe that it was - this could only mean one thing: John and Maria were not his biological parents. But there were pictures of him with his mom in the hospital birthing room; and with his dad and Renee as well. Was it really him? He thought so...so what the hell was the story? Did they do some kind of sperm donor thing, some kind of in vitro? He was confused and mad as hell. Something is really screwed up, and you never told me...What the hell is going on...

———

Coincidentally, this was the day that his mother and father, along with Renee and Paul, had chosen to tell all. They thought they had beaten what they referred to as "the dna deadline." As they sat waiting for Chris to arrive home from school, they had no idea that the horse was already out of the barn. As it was, they were collectively a bit tense as they waited, making small talk to fill the time. **Had** they known they would have realized that they had already lost control of the situation. As Paul had recently thought, the best laid plans...

Eventually the door opened and Chris came in. He looked around the room. His first take was that it was just one of their regular social gatherings. But something was not right. And something was certainly not right with Chris. In a belligerent voice he growled, "What the hell is going on?" Before anyone could respond, he said, angrily, "I just found out I'm not who I think I am, so what the hell is going on? No bullshit, mom and dad, just tell me the truth." He threw himself into an easy chair and glared at them. "Come on," he said, a little more calmly, "I'm waiting."

John ventured a hesitant question: "The dna results were confirmed?"

"No shit," Chris sneered, "How did you guess? I cannot be your biological child. You can't imagine how pissed I am to find that out at school and not from you. So, I say again, what the hell is the story?"

There were a few moments of truly deafening silence. This was not going according to plan and John was simply unable to pull himself together and respond. Paul took over.

"Chris, we came here tonight to tell you about it. We thought we'd talk to you **before** you got those dna results. Take a deep breath, Chris, give us the benefit of the doubt and listen. I'll do my best to tell you the whole story, at least as far as I know it."

"Paul, I feel like my parents have betrayed me. And now you, too? How could you do it?"

"Chris, I didn't know until a couple of days ago, and I'm here because I thought you'd be angry and that you might actually listen to me as your Godfather and your friend. And because I want to help you deal with the truth, once you know it all. So will you cool down a little and just listen?"

Chris nodded, sullenly, but he was quiet. He would listen to Paul.

"OK. The simple answer to your question is that neither your mom nor your dad was fertile. They tried having children for years and they were running out of time. So they obtained genetic material, which happened to be of middle eastern origin, and your mother underwent in vitro under Renee's medical supervision. You are, in fact, a child of your mother's womb, a true love child of your parents, but you simply do not share their dna."

"So why not ever tell me? Is what they did wrong?" He looked over at Maria and John. "You should have just told me."

Paul answered. "They didn't tell you because there's more to the story. Because they love you more than anything in the world and they didn't want to risk hurting you or your relationship with them."

"Well, I'd say they've done a pretty good job of screwing that up, but I guess I can understand where they were coming from..."

Paul interrupted. "You haven't heard the whole story yet, Chris, and we think you should hear it. Then you can decide what to do, if you decide to do anything at all. Or you can just try to tuck it all away and go about life as it has been for the last 21 years or so...But I'll leave it up to you. Do you want to know more, or are you satisfied with what I've already told you?"

"How bad can it be? Let's hear it..."

So Paul explained how he had met his folks and Renee in Europe so long ago, how they had extracted dna from what might very well have been the cloth that covered Jesus' face when he was taken down from the cross and how their goal had been simply to try to understand who the man Jesus was. To this point, they had the blessing of the Pope himself, and at this point Paul dropped out of the picture. He stayed in Rome while the others returned to Boston.

"The rub, Christian, is that your dad used that dna to create you. You are literally a clone of that man who walked the Earth 2000 years ago."

"Oh my Holy God!" Chris was stunned. "Who the hell am I?" he cried out in pain.

"You are Christian Baptista," Paul said quietly. "You have always been Christian Baptistia. You are who you are, Chris. Maybe you need a little time to think about it and confirm it in your own mind, son..."

"Holy shit! This is just too frigging much. I'm outta here. He jumped to his feet, moved quickly to the door, and slammed it behind him.

He left silence in his wake. Finally, John spoke up. "That went well," he said.

CHAPTER 36

After Chris stormed off, the four adults remained. Not much was said. There seemed to be an unspoken agreement that they would stay together until Chris returned. After awhile, Maria said, to no one in particular, "I knew this would be a disaster. " She looked over at her husband. "He hates us, John. We've lost our son."

"I don't think so, hon. He loves us. He'll understand and he'll be back." He reached over and took Maria's hand in his.

Renee had said nothing from the time Chris entered the house until this moment. She had pressed them to provide their son with the truth, and now that they had done it, her best friends, John and Maria, were suffering. Chris was suffering. She sensed their feelings of guilt and abandonment. She knew Chris felt angry and betrayed. It had not gone at all as she had hoped. She got up from her chair, walked over to John and Maria and whispered, "I'm sorry."

"No need to be sorry, Renee," said John. "We all agreed that it was the right thing to do. We owed it to him. I'm just afraid the reckoning was overdue. But I do believe it will be alright..."

Paul said, "I did my best. Under the circumstances, it was the best we **could** do. I know that boy. He's very smart, very rational, very emotionally stable. He'll figure it out. Just give him a little time. The greatest gift is love and you two and Christian share it in abundance. He'll be back."

But he did not come back. Not that night, or the next night or the one after that. Maria was becoming frantic. Where was her son? What was he doing? Would he harm himself? Please, please, Chris, call home. John was equally concerned, but he redirected his anxiety into attending to Maria. She **was** there, and she needed him. There was nothing he could do about Chris until Chris was ready. Chris ignored their calls and messages and remained missing. He never called home.

But on the third night he **did** call Paul.

"Hi, Paul. It's Chris. I'm okay. Please let my parents know. Thank you." And he hung up.

Paul called John and Maria and let them know he'd talked to Chris. "He's reaching out," he told them. "It will be okay. Just give him a little time."

The next afternoon he called Paul again, but the Auxiliary Bishop was immersed in Diocese business and he missed the call. There was no message. Paul was annoyed with himself when he saw the missed call and caller id. He had been praying for Chris. He cared deeply for the young man, and he hoped the missed call would not undermine their connection. He dialed Chris' number and, to Paul's relief, Chris answered on the 2nd ring.

"Hi, Paul. Thanks for calling back."

"Hello, Chris. Where are you?"

"Out in the wilderness and all alone."

"What? Are you okay?"

"Not really. I'm just really mad and really confused. The only one I trust right now is you. I don't even trust myself. I don't think I know who I am anymore."

"I can certainly understand how you feel, Chris. You **can** trust me. We can talk..."

"That might work. But right now I just need to be alone for awhile. That's what I wanted you to know. But I will call back, I promise. Thanks, Paul." He hung up.

Chris **was** alone, wandering through the wilderness of his thoughts. But in reality he was sitting on the deck of a summer cottage on Cape Cod, gazing absently out at the water. The cottage belonged to a school friend's family, and this time of year it was unoccupied. His friend had met him there, let him in and told him he had permission to stay there awhile as long as he took care not to mess it up. The several adjoining houses overlooking the dunes and the Bay beyond were all vacant. The beach, too, was empty but for an occasional dog walker and a flock of sea birds. The house itself was relatively small: A couple of bedrooms, kitchen, bath and living room. It was furnished with all the basic amenities. The start of the tourist season was more than a month away, so there would be no intrusions on his privacy. For the first time since that night at home, he felt his anger beginning to ebb. "My God," he thought. "Who the hell am I?" Before he left this place, he would find out.

Back in Boston, life went unavoidably on. Routines were maintained. John and Maria went to work, Renee called them frequently to provide her support and ask for any news, and Paul thought to contact a friend of his at Harvard to let them know that Chris was involved in a domestic crisis and he would need a short leave from his studies. The grief, the anxiety and the anticipation was carried along just under the surface. They would all cope somehow until Chris came back home. Paul assured them repeatedly that Chris was okay and promised to be in touch. He would surely return soon.

That night he did return, in a manner of speaking. Maria was awakened from a sound sleep by the touch of a hand on her face. It was Christian, standing beside the bed. She closed her eyes for a moment, warming to his touch. When she opened them, she saw her son, but now garbed as Jesus, his hair long, his beard short and pointed. He smiled at her and she felt a growing sense of inner peace. She closed her eyes again to allow herself to be enveloped by that feeling. She realized he was telling her that it was alright. When she opened her eyes again, she was fully awake and he was gone. In but a moment, Maria slipped back into a deep and untroubled sleep. It was the first time she had slept soundly since that night...

CHAPTER 37

C hris hardly knew where to begin. He had been absolutely furious when he slammed the door behind him the other night. He was still fuming, but at least now he had it under control enough to reflect on it. It ocurred to him that as long as he was angry he wouldn't be able to think about anything else, and there was certainly plenty to think about. What had fueled the explosion within him that had burst out of control? Betrayal was at the top of the list. The trust built up over a lifetime lost in an instant. His confidence in who he was, his whole identity, shot to hell in a few seconds. And finding out the way he did - first the dna and **only** then did they tell him. He had started out as a goddamned experiment! He was **different** from every other human being on earth, unnatural. He felt his anger begin to well up again. "Jesus Christ" he muttered. Then he caught himself and chuckled grimly at the irony. He could bloody well be talking about himself...

He decided to take a walk on the beach. It was mid-morning and the sun was rising and warming the spring air. There were a few puffy white clouds scattered across the sky. The knee-high waves broke and washed rhythmically ashore, then ran back out sweeping bits of seawood and shell along with them. There were no ships or sails visible, nothing to spoil the view as he looked out to the horizon. Down the beach, in the distance, he could see the beginnings of the salt marsh, with tall grasses waving gently in a light breeze. It was beautiful and tranquil. The anger within him began to recede like the tide, hardly noticeable at ebb, but eventually revealing a whole new beach of smooth, cool sand, speckled with interesting things. Now he could begin, at least, to deal with his anger.

As he walked slowly along the shore, he began to think more clearly. He remembered all the wonderful things he had done with his parents, the countless things they had done for him. In his entire life, he could remember not one single incident when they had hurt him. Not one. That's probably what makes this betrayal so damned painful, he thought. He thought of his mother's love. He visualized her face, her smile, her touch and he felt goosebumps run up and down his arms. His father's image drifted into his mental picture. Holding hands with mom. He was so kind, so rational, a near-perfect dad. Christian loved them both. The three of them had lived a life woven through and through with love. So why didn't they tell him? Then it struck him like a physical blow. The answer was obvious. They **did** tell him. They were willing to risk their lives in a figurative but very real way, to tell him the truth. And it followed that they had not told him before because he wasn't ready. He had been a child and would not have understood. They had not told him out of love, to protect him. But, hell, they could have waited a couple of months until he'd graduated - this was, after all, pretty traumatic stuff. But they couldn't wait, could they? The damned dna test forced their hand. In the end, what did it matter anyway? He was really their son; they were really his mom and dad. Wasn't he reacting like a child? Grow up. Get over it...It is time...

He had reached the edge of the salt marsh. He took a deep, cleansing breath of the fresh sea air. He exhaled slowly as he took in the scene before him. It was almost primeval. No people, no human sounds, not even the sound of the sea. Just acres of mud flats, separated by rivulets of ocean water, populated with a few birds and some marsh grass. Stillness prevailed. For a moment he felt transported into a distant past. He stood, entranced, until the sound of a commercial airliner passing overhead pulled him back. He turned and began to walk back down the beach.

The beach remained empty before him. He was the solitary figure to be seen, should anyone else be watching. He followed the footsteps he had left earlier as he made his way back toward the house. He thought of the poem, "Footsteps In The Sand." Who was carrying whom, he mused. Then he thought of the Zen story about the two monks who came to a river crossing. There was a young girl unable to cross. One monk picked the girl up and carried her over, set her down, and the two monks continued on their way. That night, at a monastery, the one monk asked the other, "Why did you pick that girl up? You know it is against the rules to touch a female." The other monk replied, "I left the girl back at the river. Why are you still carrying her?" Perhaps it was time to go home. He'd sleep on it and decide in the morning...

That night, Christian had the first of several visitors. Paul McCormack appeared in full Bishop's regalia. He said, "We've had many discussion about God, about faith and belief. You must now understand that the very words we use to describe god are a human creation and therefore limited by the limitations of the human mind." Then, oddly, he began to sing an old Beatles song. "Turn off your mind, relax and float down stream, it is not dying...then you'll know the meaning of within...it is shining..." Chris woke, and Paul was gone. He had trouble getting back to sleep. For some reason, the ghosts of Dickens' Christmas Carol were haunting **him** this night...

In the morning he was greeted with another strange happening. He had gone out onto the deck to watch the sun rising above the bay. In the far distance, he saw a figure - a man, walking on the water toward him. The sun was bright, shining directly into Chris' eyes.

It had to be some kind of optical illusion. He blinked, held his eyes tightly closed, opened them. The man was still there, closer and clearer now. And then he was gone. Chris shook his head and went back inside.

Later that day, Chris called Paul. He told Paul that he had come to grips with his anger. That it was gone, that as Paul had so often told him, love would conquer...and it had. But he was not ready to come home yet. He was still struggling with a truly unique identity crisis. Tell his mom and dad he loved them and that he understood. He just wasn't ready to talk to them. He just had to be alone for awhile longer. And then he said something that stuck the Bishop as unusual for Chris: "Pray for me, Paul." And then he was gone.

That evening, Chris stood on the deck, leaning on the railing, as the sun set behind him. It was dusk and the visible world was slowly fading into darkness. A light, far out on the Bay, caught his attention. It was moving toward him. He watched it as it crept along at a snail's pace. It grew larger and brighter, but no clearer. He remembered the vision he had had that morning - yes, it must have been only that, he thought - and he couldn't help wondering if he was seeing that same man here in the twilight. Then the light went out. It was getting cold. Chris shook his head and went inside.

CHAPTER 38

C hris returned home the next day. He had been away for barely more than a week, but it was a different young man who came in through the door than the one who had so angrily slammed it behind him when he had gone. He knew. He understood. He was genuinely okay. Now he wanted to be sure his parents were okay, too. It was Saturday and Maria and John were home when he walked in. They were simultaneously surprised, relieved and thrilled to see him. He hurried over to them and embraced them both. All three felt tears welling up as they hugged. Chris said, "I love you," and, for the moment, that was enough.

Later, they sat and talked. Chris told them where he had been but not everything that had happened there. He simply said he had gotten over his anger and that he understood everything. He did not reveal that he now thought he understood it better than they did. Enough revelations for the the time being. Maybe he would tell them later. At the moment it was enough to let them know that he appreciated why they had not told him before and now that he knew...well, he could live with it. That part about where the genetic material came from - let's just forget it. It's enough for me to know that I am your physical child, mom, and you're mom's husband and my dad. Paul told me love is the most important thing, and I realized that he's right. I've had it and given it in this family my whole life and there's no reason to change that now.

For their part, Maria and John spoke of their regrets. They should never have used the donor material they did. They should never have attempted a human cloning. They should have done in vitro with a known and acceptable sperm donor. They should have told Chris sooner. But in spite of all they had done that was wrong, they still had a wonderful son. And now he was back home, accepting and forgiving. The same loving son as before. Chris thought, "Perhaps not quite the same." But this was surely not a moment to quibble; it was a time to heal. Telling them the rest of the story might be a disaster...

The family spent the remainder of the day together, sharing memories and repairing the bonds. It was a good thing for all of them. Maria made dinner and they continued to talk and reminisce as they ate. Later they relaxed in the living room, watched a little TV, and dozed off in their chairs. It had been a very long and exhausting day...

For Christian, the next day would be longer and harder. He had chosen to keep much of what had happened on the Cape from his parents. They didn't need to know. There was, however, one person who absolutely **had** to be told the rest of the story. In fact, the story could not continue to its conclusion without his intervention. Chris picked up the phone and called Paul McCormack. He told the Bishop he was home, that things were fine with his folks, and he needed to talk about something very important. Paul said he was delighted to hear that Chris was back. He told Chris that he had Sunday services to attend to but he had no commitments for the rest of the afternoon and he invited him to come on over.

When Chris met Paul he got right to the point. He told him about his visions and his revelations: How Jesus had appeared to him, how Mary had spoken to him, how Paul himself had appeared in a dream. He recounted what they had said to him. And he told the Bishop that he now believed he **was** Jesus' genetic twin and that he was created, in part, to fulfill a mission. His mission was to be a messenger to the Pope. He was to represent Jesus - no, part of him was to **be** Jesus - and personally deliver that message to John Paul III in Rome. The Pontiff had initiated this meeting himself, when he sent a young Father Paul McCormack on a very private and secret quest. The last thing Jesus had said to Chris was, "It is time..."

Up to that point, Paul had listened, interested, perhaps intrigued, but unconvinced. In fact, he was beginning to become concerned about Chris' mental status. This young man was his friend and his Godson, and the possibility that the shock of learning his true biological history might have provoked hallucinatory dementia seemed to Paul to be very real. Chris probably needed clinical help. After all, all the facts necessary for his mind to conjuring up these visions and revelations were already in his possession. All but the last. When Chris said, "It is time," Paul was first startled and then dumbfounded. Only he, Auxiliary Bishop Paul McCormack, knew the words that John Paul III had heard in his dream - the words that had initially launched Paul and the others on their quest. The words that ultimately resulted in the birth of Christian Baptista! It was either one hell of a coincidence, or there was the possibility that Christian had been conceived by design and was now being guided by holy visitations and revelations. He remembered once telling Chris that miracles are all around us. Perhaps this was one of them...

Paul asked Chris what he planned to say to the Pope. Chris replied that he didn't know. He was simply a messenger and the words would be spoken by Jesus directly to His Holiness. As a Bishop, Paul thought there was a real risk of heresy here - a man speaking as and claiming to be the embodiment of Christ. Why would Jesus not speak directly to the Pope? Why go through the trouble of creating a clone and raising him up to maturity before revealing his mission? Then, again, if Chris' visions and revelations were genuine, who was he to question what God was about? After all, as he had often been told (and said more than a few times himself) the Lord works in strange ways.

Paul shared his thoughts, directly and honestly, with Chris. While he was not willing to embrace Chris' story unconditionally, he was able to accept it as divinely inspired. He did so not only as Christian's confidant, but also as a Bishop in the service of God and the Church. He asked Chris what he wanted to do. "Why, go to Rome, of course," he replied

---

Over the next days, Paul McCormack made an unusual and extraordinary effort to communicate with the Pontiff. He was hampered by the fact that he could tell no one but the Pope himself what the message was. He had promised total secrecy all those many years ago and he had no intention of breaking that vow now. The message he wanted to send was simple: "It is time. I humbly request an immediate private audience with Your Holiness." He tried normal channels only to find that messages from Auxiliary Bishops were unlikely to reach the Pontiff, and that if they actually arrived in the hands of the Papal Secretary it would be some considerable time before one received a response. That response was likely to be from the Secretary and almost certainly a rejection of the request. After a fruitless week, he made a decision. They would fly to Rome and seek an audience in person.

CHAPTER 39

A couple of days later, Auxiliary Bishop Paul McCormack and Christian Baptista flew to Rome. Paul had taken a few days leave to go on a personal pilgrimage. Chris had told his parents that he had the opportunity of a lifetime - to accompany Paul on a visit to the Vatican. Maria was thrilled for him; John not so much, because it meant more time away from Harvard. But he did think it would be an eye-opening educational opportunity, so he acquiesced. Besides, he saw no point in making a serious objection that might result in reigniting a confrontation with Chris. Better to just let them go....and they did.

Their flight took them over the Gulf of Naples on a full-moon night. The waves below them reflected the silvery light and looked as motionless as a still photograph. It was a memorable sight. The plane seemed to follow a path of moonlight laid down on the surface of the sea, and before long they had descended and set down on the runway at Leonardo DaVinci Airport. Bishop McCormack passed quickly through customs and immigration, taking Chris along with him. They collected their light travel bags and caught the train for Rome. A half hour later they were downtown. They took a cab to the Vatican and were very soon settling into a small, but comfortable, guest room in a building reserved as a domicile for visiting prelates.

The following morning, Chris woke to find that Paul was already up and out. He made a cup of coffee and sat with it, thinking about what he would say to the Pope. He had no idea. But he was not anxious in the least, because he **knew** that someone else would be doing the talking. All he really needed to do was to get an audience.

There was a gentle knock on the door, the knob turned and Paul walked in, dressed in work-a-day clothing. He had left his message at the office of the Papal Secretary. Now all they could do was to wait and hope that the Pontiff would see them. Chris had no doubt that there would be an audience. And he was right. They didn't have to wait very long. There was a sharp knock at the door, and Paul opened it to find a uniformed Swiss Guardsman, who confirmed that he was in the presence of Bishop McCormack, and having been satisfied, handed Paul a small, sealed envelope. He saluted and departed. Paul carefully unsealed and opened the envelope. Inside was a small card bearing the official seal of John Paul III. On it was written "Private Audience with His Holiness, 2 p.m. today." It was signed by the Pope's personal secretary. Paul was, of course, quite pleased. He'd managed to arrange the meeting. But he was also hit, suddenly, with a gut-wrenching anxiety attack. Had he done the right thing? How would this play out before the highest and most powerful leader in Christiandom? Chris put his arm around Paul and said, "It is time. It will be fine." And somehow Paul felt better, reassured. He simply **knew** Christian was right.

At precisely 2 o'clock, they were ushered into the Pope's private residence. Paul was wearing appropriate clerical garb. He had been here before and the place looked little changed from what he remembered. John Paul III, however, had changed dramatically. He was no longer the vital looking and strong middle aged leader he had been then. He was now an old man, looking tired and worn. But he was still the same kind and gentle - and now much-beloved - Holy

Father. He sat in his large, red leather chair and motioned them toward him. Paul knelt and kissed the Pontiff's ring; Chris followed Paul's example. John Paul looked at Chris with some curiosity, but he said nothing. He motioned for his visitors to sit.

He said, "I remember you, Father McCormack. It has been quite a long time, but I well remember. You have served us well."

"Thank you, Your Holiness."

"I did not anticipate an additional guest. Tell me, please. Why is he here?"

Paul had thought about this moment long and hard, and now he answered very carefully.

"Your Holiness, this young man is Christian Baptista. He is the son of the scientists you employed to study certain holy relics. He has reported to me visions and revelations of a unique nature. I believe they may be consequential to your original charge to me and I felt compelled to bring them to your attention."

"Yes, I understood from your request for a private audience that it concerned that matter. Tell me briefly what he has seen and heard."

"He has been visited by the person of Jesus on several occasions, and he has spoken with the Lord and been spoken to by Mother Mary."

"And were there revelations?"

"Yes, Holiness."

"And do you know the substance of these revelations?"

"No, Holiness. Only that the Lord wishes to speak directly to you, and that this young man believes he is the messenger."

"And you have faith in Christian?"

"Yes, Holiness. I have known him his entire life. I am his Godfather. I know the special circumstances of his origins." Paul was afraid that the Pope might enquire abut that last remark, but he did not, so Paul continued. "And, Holiness, his visitors told him 'It is time.' That is why I brought him to you."

"I see," said the Pope. "You may withdraw, Father, and await in the outer room. Leave me for awhile with Christian."

Paul rose, knelt briefly before the Pontiff, and quietly departed. The Pope looked over at Christian with a kindly expression and said, "Alright, young man, I am ready to hear your message..."

"I am Him and I am not Him. You caused me to be re-created in body and mind, but you could not recreate the divine. That part of me is but a visitation and I shall soon depart. It is **not** my time. It is **your** time and I have come to tell you what you want to know."

"Tell me, then, so that I may judge the truth for myself."

"You are a good and holy man. You are a pastor, not a king. You do the best you can in this time and place. Much of what you do is flawed, but you are a man, and you are forgiven. Your good works will be rewarded."

"I am much saddened and disappointed in what I see. I gave Peter the keys to the Kingdom of Heaven. Those keys have too often been ill-used by his successors. Were I of a mind to, I'd ask you to give them back. But much good has been done, and I cannot, in any case, un-do 2000 years of human history."

"The church I imagined was a spiritual association of faith. What I find is an institution that looks like Imperial Rome. It is rigid and full of pride. It sees itself as the arbiter of truth and has created orthodoxy and heresy where none should exist."

"The Church has inserted itself between the people and God, in the guise of a holy intermediary."

" You have created Saints and elevated them to heavenly status."

"You come perilously close to idolatry, especially when you elevate my Earthly mother to an exalted status."

"You have conducted wars, sponsored intolerance, murdered heretics."

"In spite of elevating Mother Mary, you have otherwise demoted women to permanent subservience."

"Your cannon is flawed. Much of what is in it is not right. Some of what is not in it, should be. And this flawed cannon is not **my** word, but the words of men. Upon this you base your orthodoxy."

"The Apocalypse is a series of visions and prophecies foreign to me."

"Most of all, the Church has frequently lost its humanity. Children have been abused and it has been tolerated. Evil and powerful men have received approbation and even the Church's support. This is intolerable and damnable. More recently, you and your immediate predecessors have acted to curb these and many other wrongs, and to minister to the poor and needy. For this, I applaud you.

"The Church I see is not the one I imagined. But it **is** a human institution and therefore cannot avoid being flawed. I recognize the good that has been done and, on balance, the good outweighs the ills. I have come to task you with considering these things I have told you, and to dedicate yourself to making your church better, making it more human, more pastoral, more ecumenical. Make it truly **my** church, as it was long ago."

He had no sooner completed this last admonition when Christian collapsed and fell to the floor.

CHAPTER 40

C hrisitian was transported by ambulance, unconcious, to a hospital in Rome. Paul McCormack rode with him and was by his side when he was admitted through the emergency room. He remained unconcious while the medical staff attempted to determine what was wrong. They were told that Chris was a tourist who had fallen in the Vatican and apparently hit his head on the hard floor. That was perfectly consistent with their findings, a bit of intracranial swelling, a few cc of internal bleeding. They put him on a mild IV anticoagulant to prevent clotting and an anti-inflamatory to manage the swelling. And then all that they could do was to wait. Christian would be fine, they told Paul, it would just be a matter of time until he woke up. Paul dutifully notified Maria and John that Chris had had an accident, and explained his condition. It was not life threatening and the doctors anticipated that he would recover quickly, probably long before his parents could book a flight and get to Rome themselves. He suggested that they sit tight, and he would be home with Chris in a day or two. If anything changed, he would let them know.

Meanwhile, Chris **was** conscious of one final visitation. He knew somehow that it was the last he would experience in his lifetime. Jesus sat beside his bed and held his hand. He didn't speak a word, but Chris was pleasantly surprised that he understood the message. He had done well. Now there would be no more to do. He would be free to live a normal life. He would forget all that had happened.

217

The audience had been between Jesus and the Pope. Chris had been a mere observer and now he must forget, forget in order to be free... and as Jesus faded away, so did the memories. When he opened his eyes, they were gone. Instead of Jesus, there was, of all people, Paul McCormack, seated at his side. Chris was disoriented. He had no idea what he was doing in this bed, or, for that matter, where in the world he was. He asked Paul, "What happened?"

"You don't remember?"

"Not a thing."

"We're in the hospital, Chris. We were visiting the Vatican and you fell and hit your head. Do you remember that?"

"Not at all."

"What **do** you remember, son?"

Chris thought for a moment. "The last thing I remember is dinner with my folks..."

Just as well, thought Paul. Then he said, "Let's call your folks. Then let's get out of here and head for home..."

———

When they arrived at Logan Airport, John and Maria were there to greet them. There were hugs and kisses all around, and Maria fussed with Chris' hair and clothing, as moms are want to do. Little was said as they drove home through the Boston traffic. Paul and Chris were obviously exhausted, and Maria and John respected their silence. Plenty of time for talk later. They dropped Paul off at the Diocese, then headed back toward their own place. While John parked the car, Maria and Chris walked together up to the front door, opened it and went inside. Chris hugged his mother. He kissed her gently and said, "Mom, it is **so good** to be home. Maria glanced upward and whispered "Thank you, Mary," and to Chris she said, simply, "I love you."

EPILOGUE

C hristian returned to Harvard and completed his Thesis. He graduated at the end of the summer. His paper concluded with an observation and a challenge:

"Whether God created man or man created God is really not the most challenging question. The two views are inherently connected, like the chicken and the egg. For much of human history, God has been viewed by man as the creator, the author of an orderly universe, variously angry or forgiving, usually interventionist, the symbol of the unimaginable and the inexplicable and the phenomenological first cause. Arguably, all of these things are in one way or another a projection of our humanness. But that does not preclude the existence of a God with those attributes. It could be argued that we believe as we do because God made us that way. But now we are on the verge of a new human era, an era in which **man** can create man, not in the way it has always been done, but with the deliberate intent of genetic manipulation. Who knows what we will create or how different that creation may become from what we have for so long been. Who knows what the consequences will be for mankind? And who knows, in turn, what the consequences will be for our relationship with God? As we face this indeterminate future, have we the ability to apply the wisdom of the past to the a world of **our own** creation? Will we have a place for God, or will we supplant Him? And if He is real and present, what will He do? The unavoidable challenge of the future is whether belief and science are indeed married, or if science will ultimately give birth to a belief system that is entirely new. On such questions rest the future of mankind."